J. T. EDSON'S
FLOATING OUTFIT

The toughest bunch of Rebels that ever lost a war, they fought for the South, and then for Texas, as the legendary Floating Outfit of "Ole Devil" Hardin's O.D. Connected ranch.

MARK COUNTER was the best-dressed man in the West: always dressed fit-to-kill. **BELLE BOYD** was as deadly as she was beautiful, with a "Manhattan" model Colt tucked under her long skirts. **THE YSABEL KID** was Comanche fast and Texas tough. And the most famous of them all was **DUSTY FOG**, the ex-cavalryman known as the Rio Hondo Gun Wizard.

J. T. Edson has captured all the excitement and adventure of the raw frontier in this magnificent Western series. Turn the page for a complete list of Berkley Floating Outfit titles.

J.T. Edson
THE TEXAN

BERKLEY BOOKS, NEW YORK

Originally printed in Great Britain by
Brown Watson Limited.

This Berkley book contains the complete
text of the original edition.
It has been completely reset in a typeface
designed for easy reading, and was printed
from new film.

THE TEXAN

A Berkley Book / published by arrangement with
Transworld Publishers, Ltd.

PRINTING HISTORY
Brown Watson edition published 1962
Corgi edition published 1968
Berkley edition / March 1983

ISBN: 0–425–05858–1

A BERKLEY BOOK ® TM 757,375
Berkley Books are published by Berkley Publishing Corporation,
200 Madison Avenue, New York, New York 10016.
The name ''BERKLEY'' and the stylized ''B'' with design are
trademarks belonging to Berkley Publishing Corporation.
PRINTED IN THE UNITED STATES OF AMERICA

CHAPTER ONE

A Case Of Mistaken Identity

"Give me back that scalp!"

The words, yelled in a schoolboy's treble, came to Marshal Jack Mollison as he walked the Main Street of Tensonville, New Mexico. For a moment he stood listening to the yelling and scuffling, then walked in between two houses to investigate.

The two fighting boys separated as they saw the lean, angular form of the Marshal bearing down on them. Mollison was a respected and well-liked lawman in this town. True, he did not present the eye-catching appearance of either Wyatt Earp nor the late, but not overly-lamented Wild Bill Hickok. Not for him the expensively-tailored clothes, the shiny town shoes, or the easily-greased palm. No one ever presented him with a long-barrelled gun as either a token of respect, or in the Texas view, payment for services rendered. Rather he looked like the foreman of a ranch with his range clothes, and, even after several years of Peacemaker production, he still clung to his old Colt 1860 Army revolver.

For a moment, Mollison thought the object one of the boys held was a scalp. It came as a relief to see it was only a well-made wig of red hair.

"I found it. That makes it mine, don't it, Mr. Mollison?" one of the pair asked.

"Waal, now, happen you find an unrecorded gold

strike, or a steer without a brand, it's yours. But if you find something like money, or that thing, it isn't. That's the law—don't ask me why, but that's it."

The boy reluctantly handed over the wig. "I allus wanted a real scalp. Wonder who it belongs to?"

Mollison was wondering just the same thing. To the best of his knowledge, no man in town wore a wig of any kind; and there were not many red-headed men in this section. He turned the wig over in his hands; but on the inside there was nothing to help identify its owner.

"Where'd you find it?" he asked.

"Out back of the Vent Bar," the boy replied, still eyeing the wig wistfully. "Can't I have it?"

"Law says I have to hold it for a spell, to give the owner a chance to come in and claim it. So I'll just have to hold on to it down at the jail. But any reward I get for it I'll give you." Mollison watched the disappointed face and dug out a quarter to pass it across to the youngster. "Here's something on account."

This satisfied the two youngsters. They walked away together, their fight forgotten. Mollison watched them go, then looked at the wig again, and went along to his office. Inside the small room, he went to the safe, opened it and threw the wig inside. Locking the door he went back to his desk and took out a sheaf of reports sent out by the Texas Rangers. These reports covered the activities of various outlaw gangs. The one he wanted was on top.

"The Shotgun Gang," it read. "No known members. Number of gang usually four or five. No adequate descriptions of any members. One is small with red hair. Others are all tall."

The report went on to list the various stage hold-ups this gang was responsible for; and the fact that, although they wore hand-guns, their main line of defence were the ten-gauge shotguns they always carried.

Standing up, Mollison walked across the room and out into the street. He stood there for a moment, looking first up towards Pop Howard's livery barn, then in the opposite direction at the post office. Finally, his eyes took in the front of the Vent Bar, Tensonville's only saloon. The paint of the name was still new-looking, compared with the other buildings. This was because Barry Vent was not long in this town, having won the business in a poker game from its previous owner six months back.

The Marshal loosed his old gun in the holster and stepped forward out across the street. He went on to the opposite sidewalk and stepped along until he could see into the bar. It was dimly-lit and there were only five men inside. He pushed open the batwing doors and looked the five over. Four were the saloon's hired hands; the fifth, a handsome, dandy-dressed young man belting a brace of silver-mounted Colts, was Benjy Vent, brother of the owner.

It was the four men who interested Mollison—for he knew Benjy Vent to be a swaggering bully, trouble-causer and coward, who would have been cut down long since, without the backing of his brother's toughs.

Two of the four were tall and thin, the other two short and stocky. The tall pair were Brandon, a gangling beanpole who wore range clothes and served behind the bar, and Wheeler, a town-dressed Missourian who acted as a waiter. The short couple were a bald hardcase called Shorty Smith and a red-haired, flashily-dressed dude waiter known as Haines. These four, along with a killer called Slingo Witch, were Barry Vent's entire staff, a clannish bunch who got on with themselves and made no attempt to become friendly with anyone in town.

"Howdy, Marshal," Smith said as he polished the bartop with a cloth. "We don't see much of you in here."

"Don't often see you four all in here at one time,

either," Mollison answered—thinking that, when Barry Vent or Slingo Witch were absent, it was always Smith who did the talking.

"Trade's never enough for us all four, 'cepting on payday."

"Funny thing that, last pay-night there wasn't but the two of you in here," Mollison remarked.

"Yes, there was," Smith was just a shade too quick off the mark. "We worked in two shifts—right boys?"

"What're you getting at Marshal?" Vent asked.

"Nothing much—except that, mebbe, you've been too long in this town. Happen you stop. I might start thinking things."

"What sort of things?"

"Like how, if you put a wig on Smith and dressed him up, he'd be mistook for Haines—especially if he was around the tables, instead of behind the bar."

"What're you accusing us of?" Benjy Vent snarled.

"Nothing, just asking. One thing though, sonny. Keep away from my daughter—she doesn't want any part of you."

"Yeah?" Benjy sneered and moved forward, his hands hovering near the butts of his guns. "Who says so?"

Mollison back-handed the young man hard, spinning him into the bar. Then he followed it up with a right to his stomach, which doubled Benjy over. The youngster went to his knees, holding his stomach and moaning, not offering to either get up or fight back. Smith looked over and snarled deep in his throat angrily. Mollison came round and snapped:

"What'd you say?"

"Barry Vent ain't going to like this, Mollison. He'll be wanting to see you."

"Tell him I'll be waiting by that cottonwood just outside town. And tell him to come himself, not to send his hired killer."

"I'll tell him, Mollison, I'll tell him," Smith answered. "He'll likely be along to see you."

After the Marshal left, Smith came round the bar and dragged Benjy to his feet. With anger and contempt curling his lips, the small man snarled, "I'm quick getting sick of you and your mouth. Barry's told you to keep your fool trap shut and let me do all the talking when the law comes round."

Barry Vent and his men lived in a small house next door to the saloon. It was owned by a widow who worked at the eating-house and was never at home during the day. Smith and Benjy entered and went upstairs to the room Barry Vent used for himself and his constant companion—the killer, Slingo Witch.

Barry Vent looked up from the letter he was reading when Smith and his brother entered. He noted Benjy's dishevelled clothes and asked, "What happened?"

Smith looked the two men over. Vent was tall, handsome and dressed in the height of frontier gambling fashion. Even in the house, he wore a glove on his right hand; Smith had never seen him without a glove on. Slingo Witch was also tall, lean and his face was hard, cold and emotionless. He wore range clothes, dark in colour and untidy, only the gunbelt with the matched guns was cared for in his appearance.

"Mollison came into the saloon and got to asking questions. Then Benjy here started sassing him. I reckon the Marshal's getting suspicious," Smith replied.

Barry Vent looked hard at his brother and then back at Smith. Benjy scowled defiance back, but was nervous. He knew that Slingo Witch would kill him if he gave him half a chance out. He jerked a thumb towards Smith and snapped:

"This hard man didn't help me. Him and the rest just stood by while Mollison hit me."

"He didn't hit you hard enough," Barry barked back. "I've warned you about getting flip with Mollison and to stay clear of his girl. He's not the sort of man to stand for any big-mouth talk from you. The girl doesn't want you and the blacksmith is keen on her. You keep fooling round and we'll get bad trouble.''

''We've got it now,'' Smith put in. ''Mollison got to saying how me and Bud Haines looked alike. Then this loud mouth here had to ask him what he was accusing us of.''

''The Marshal's getting all suspicious, is he?'' Slingo Witch asked, his voice a soft purr, his hands as always near to his gun-butts.

''Yeah, allows we've been round here too long. Say's he'll be waiting to see you under that cottonwood there, and for you to come alone, Barry.'' Smith watched Barry Vent's face all the time, remembering he'd never seen the gambler either use or hold a gun.

''Sure'd hate to see a man disappointed, Barry,'' Slingo Witch's voice showed no feeling. He rose with a little move and went to the window, looking out.

Across the street, and through a gap in between the opposite houses, Witch could see the cottonwood tree, and, under it, the tall shape of the Marshal. Barry Vent came to stand by the other man's side, looking down also. He turned and came back to face his brother and Smith.   .

''Listen, and listen good, you two. I've heard from our friend with Wells Fargo. There's a shipment on a stage through here in the near future. We're going to take it when he sends us the telegraph message. Until then, I don't want any trouble at all. I'm going to settle Mollison right now. Smith, you take Benjy to the saloon and keep him there.''

Smith nodded. He walked to the door and jerked his head to Benjy, who followed him out of the room. Slingo Witch watched them go, then went to the closet and opened the door to take something out, saying: ''You go ahead and see the Marshal.''

Jack Mollison watched the gambler walking towards him. His challenge was getting better results than he'd hoped for. It was only on the off-chance that he had given out the challenge, for he had not thought that Barry Vent would come out here and face him down. His suspicions were correct; Barry Vent did have something to hide. It was something which kept him running a small saloon in this out-of-the-way town, making a small profit when he could have been in some far larger and more affluent location.

Vent halted, standing with legs apart, hand hovering over the butt of his fancy pearl-handled Remington revolver. He looked around. There was no one near; down at the livery barn, Mollison's father-in-law, Pop Howard, was working in the corral, but was not looking this way.

"I hear you've been asking my boys some questions," Vent said.

"Sure—and, from the way they acted, I reckon it's time you moved on."

"Meaning?"

"From now on, I'm going to keep a real careful watch on your place, and make sure who's there. That way, I don't reckon the Shotgun Gang will ride again."

Silence fell, neither man saying a word as they watched each other. At last, Barry Vent spoke: "You know too much!"

Mollison's hand went down as Barry Vent's moved, the old 1860 Army gun coming clear of leather.

Along the street Pop Howard heard the shot, and turned. He stared, gave an angry, startled curse and, with a speed which belied his years and his bowed legs, climbed the corral fence and hurried towards the tree.

The Marshal lay on his back under the tree. In his hand his old gun was smoking. Barry Vent stood looking down at him, gun in leather. He shook his head as a crowd started to gather.

"Mollison drew on me. I had to kill him."

By that time, Slingo Witch and Smith were forcing their way through the crowd and flanking their boss. They faced the crowd, watching the tall, muscular young blacksmith and the middle-sized, bandy-legged old-timer, Pop Howard. These were the two men most likely to cause trouble. Johnny Sinclair never wore a gun, but his big hands were weapon enough. Pop Howard was not wearing his old Dragoon Colt, but he was a ringy cuss and capable of making war.

"Never knowed Jack pull first on any man," Howard growled.

"Calling the boss a liar, old man?" Slingo Witch asked.

A thin, emaciated old-timer wearing a threadbare suit and a dirty, collarless white shirt moved forward. "Pop didn't mean it that ways, Mr. Witch. Ain't none of us doubting Mr. Vent's words."

"Mollison's gun's out and smoking," Vent pointed out.

"Why'd he draw?" Johnny Sinclair asked.

"You know these old John laws," Slingo Witch answered. "They have to stack up——"

The words ended up abruptly as Johnny Sinclair lunged forward, a big fist shooting out. The killer went over backwards, smashing to the ground with both legs waving. The blacksmith started to move forward, but Pop Howard caught his arm, holding him back. The old-timer knew that Witch was out of the game; but Smith would take a hand in it, if Johnny Sinclair attacked the killer again.

"Cut it out, Johnny!" he snapped. "Go see to Jean—she'll need caring for. Two of you gent's help me to get Jack home."

Johnny Sinclair turned and walked away. Two of the men lifted the still form and followed Pop Howard towards the livery barn. Barry Vent watched them go, then turned to the crowd, looking round.

"Jack Mollison sent for me to come here and see him. When I came, he went for his gun. I didn't have a choice but to kill him."

•   •   •

The cowhand rode into Tensonville a week after the shooting. He halted the seventeen-hand paint stallion for a moment, looking along the main street, then at the bullet-pocked board which announced to all and sundry that this was the town of Tensonville, Curry County, New Mexico. For some reason, this sign made him smile; he looked like a man who was surprised to find the town at all. Kneeing the big horse gently, he allowed it to move forward, headed for Howard's livery barn.

The horse was a beauty, even with the rangeland prejudice against paints for working mounts. It was seventeen hands of uncut, thoroughbred wickedness, from its head to the long tail; not the sort of horse a beginner would chose to learn riding on—not if he wanted to live long enough to learn. It was a fine-looking horse, one which had cost plenty; somehow, the rider did not give the impression that he should own, or be riding, such a fine animal.

He was a smallish man, not more than five-foot-six; yet to anyone who looked, he was wide-shouldered and strong-looking. His low-crowned, wide-brimmed black Stetson was expensive and set back on his dusty blond-coloured hair. His face was handsome and young-looking, yet it was not a weak face. His bandana, shirt and levis were not new, being faded and well-washed; but his boots were costly, fancy-stitched, and the Kelly spurs on them were of top quality. Around his waist was a gun-belt and, in the holsters, butt forward, were a brace of white-handled, matched Colt Civilian Peacemakers.

He lounged easily in the saddle; it was a good Texas rig, low-horned and double-girthed. Behind the cantle was strapped his bedroll; to the horn, a sixty foot rope; and, from under his left leg, in its saddle-boot was a Winchester Model 73 carbine.

Johnny Sinclair and Jean Mollison were talking at the door of the livery stable when the cowhand rode leisurely towards the corral. Neither took much notice of him at first; he was not the sort who would catch the eye. Besides, they were in earnest and urgent conversation on a matter of some importance.

"Johnny boy," the girl said, "you'll get bad trouble, if you don't watch what you're doing."

The blacksmith scowled. "I'm tired of Benjy Vent hanging round you all the time—and of that bunch at the saloon insinuating that your father started the fight with Vent. I've told them that, if I hear it said again, I'll beat hell out of them."

"Then Barry Vent or Slingo Witch will kill you." The girl's voice was tender and gentle. "Leave them alone, Johnny. It isn't worth getting killed over."

Johnny Sinclair looked down at the pretty face—for Jean Mollison was a very pretty girl. Her face had never felt the touch of any make-up and was fresh, tanned and faultless. From her dainty shoes to the top of her brunette head, she was a sight to make a man look twice, even in that old gingham dress. The blacksmith towered over her, a big man wearing a sleeveless shirt, levis and a thick leather apron which showed his business in life.

He wanted to change the subject, but he wasn't a good conversationalist and wasn't sure how to go about it. The girl was over the worst of her grief at her father's death, but he did not wish to keep reminding her of it. The young cowhand was almost to the corral rail by then. Johnny watched him for a moment.

"I wonder if it's him," he said thoughtfully, then shook his head. "No, it couldn't be—this town doesn't have that kind of luck."

"Isn't *who*?" she asked.

"No, not alone it wouldn't be." Johnny was not speaking to Jean, he was deep in his own thoughts. "I'd best get back to the forge and do some work."

Jean was used to Johnny Sinclair's ways and took no offence at his sudden departure. She smiled and shook her head as she watched him walk away, then said to herself, "It's nice to know someone cares."

The door of the house opened. Pop Howard came

out, then ambled towards her. She noticed he was giving
the newcomer the same attention Johnny had used on
him. He stumped over to her and asked: "What did
Johnny want?"

Jean watched the young man swing down from his
saddle at the corral before she answered: "Just warning
me to beware of gambling men with brothers who need
a good spanking."

"Sure—and one day Johnny'll do it," Pop growled.
He gazed at the youngster, who was standing by his
paint and looking at the other horses in the corral. "I
wonder if it is him?"

"You're the second to say that. Who do you mean?"

"Dusty Fog?"

Jean stared at her grandfather for a moment before
she saw what he meant. The Rio Hondo gun-wizard,
Dusty Fog, rode a paint stallion and toted twin guns in
border-draw holsters. All too often, she'd heard about
this famous, fabulous Texan. How, in the War Between
The States, he'd been the equal of the Dixie guerilla
champions, John Singleton Mosby and Turner Ashby.
Since then, he'd got a reputation as being the equal of
such exponents of the art of "triggernometry" as Wes
Hardin, King Fisher, Ben Thompson and other wizards
of the tied-down holster.

All she'd ever heard of Dusty Fog did not fit with this
small young man in the faded clothes. This small, insignificant, unassuming-looking youngster was far from
being what she imagined in a man with a reputation like
that of Dusty Fog. She looked at those two white-
handled guns and remembered the matched brace of
gold-mounted guns Dusty Fog had won at Tombstone
in the Cochise County Fair shooting match. The Rio
Hondo gun-wizard would be wearing those guns, and
this man was not.

"He's certainly trying to prove he is," she replied.
"*Is* it him?"

"Never saw him but once, when he was about three

year old,'' Pop answered. "But all the Fog clan were tall men. Dusty's pappy tops six foot. That boy ain't him at all.''

They crossed the open space and the young man turned to greet them. His hat came off as he saw the girl.

"Mind if I leave the hoss here for a spell, friend?'' he asked, his soft voice, a pleasant Texas drawl. "Happen for a week or so. Need a place to sleep, too.''

"Leave the horse either in a stall, or at the corral. We've a spare room you can take if you like,'' Jean put in, before her grandfather could speak. She wanted to prevent this young man from going to the Vent bar; for, if he did, Slingo Witch might think he was Dusty Fog and would certainly kill him.

"Suit me fine, ma'am,'' the Texan answered. "I've been sage-henning for a week now and a man gets tired of his own fixings. You don't have a white, blood-bay and a paint here?''

"No. Would it bother you if there had been?'' Jean remembered that Dusty Fog's two inseparable friends, Mark Counter and the Ysabel Kid, rode a blood-bay and a white respectively.

"It surely would, ma'am.'' The Texan's grin made him look even more boyish than before. "I'll fix my hoss, then get my gear to the room.''

The young man loosened the clinches and worked the saddle for a time, then swung it free. He must have been far stronger than he first gave the impression of being, for he handled the heavy rig with no trouble. He stood with it over his shoulder and looked again at the other horses in the corral.

"I reckon the stall would be the best thing for us, ma'am. This ole paint of mine doesn't take to company. He's real mean with any strange horse.''

"All right,'' she answered. "I'll show you the stalls. Come with me.''

The paint walked behind its master like a huge hound-

dog and Jean led the way to the stalls. Inside the
building, she watched him send his horse into one and
follow it, to strip off the bridle. He avoided a nip from
the paint's teeth with an easy skill which showed he
knew the horse well.

"Danged fool ole goat!" he scoffed. "Don't you ever
learn?"

The girl watched the Texan with some misgivings.
This youngster could not be the famous Dusty Fog, and
most certainly should not be pretending he was. She
looked at the gun-belt and the horse; they were not what
one might expect a youngster like this to be wearing, nor
owning.

"We've a burro in the lean-to if you like to leave your
saddle there," she remarked as he dropped the bar of
the gate behind the paint.

The Texan followed her again, carrying the saddle
over his shoulder. In the lean-to was a small wooden
structure like the roof of a house. Over this, he hung his
saddle—for no cowhand ever liked leaving it on the
ground. If he did, he would lay it carefully on one side,
never standing it on its skirts. However, the saddle was
far better kept on a wooden burro.

He unstrapped the bed-roll and pulled the carbine
from its boot, then followed the girl out of the building.
Pop ambled over to the stall and looked at the big paint,
trying to read the brand. The horse was still shaggy with
winter coat and he could not see the tell-tale mark on it,
so he reached over to touch. The stallion snorted and
came round with wicked teeth bared. Pop drew back his
hand; he knew horses and knew better than to interfere
with this one.

They went across the yard and entered the small,
clean house. None of them spoke as Jean led the young
man upstairs and into the small side room. She looked
around; the bed was laid ready and there was a small
table by it with a water jug. In the corner, was a small
washstand; the Texan looked towards this and rubbed

his hand over his bristle-covered jaw.

"What did you say your name was?" she asked.

"Dusty," he answered, then stopped himself before
he said the second word.

She looked hard at him for a moment. Then she
turned and walked out of the room, to come back with a
pitcher of hot water. He'd laid his carbine on the floor
in the corner of the room and his bed-roll lay open on
the floor. He looked at a photograph on the wall and
asked: "Your pappy?"

Jean nodded and bit her lip as she looked away. The
young man didn't say another word about it as he took
the water and poured it into the bowl. She left the room,
then opened the door and looked in again.

"The meal will be ready when you've washed up,"
she said and was gone.

The Texan watched the door close, and smiled. Then
he spoke softly to himself. "You don't believe me, I
reckon. Best keep it that way and I'll surely win that
bet."

He removed the gun-belt, laying it carefully on the
bed, then stripped off his shirt and started to wash up.
He was shaving, holding the razor in his left hand, when
hoof-beats in the street attracted his attention. He went
to the window, leaving the razor on the table. Coming
back, he took the razor up with his right hand to con-
tinue shaving.

Pop Howard watched the girl come downstairs, and
asked: "Who is he?"

"A cowhand called Dusty," she replied.

Pop grunted. "You reckon he is Dusty Fog?"

"Of *course* not!" Jean was firm on that; a small, insignificant young man like that one could not possibly
be the Rio Hondo gun-wizard. "He isn't wearing those
gold-mounted guns he won at Tombstone. And he
rarely goes alone—the Ysabel Kid and Mark Counter
are nearly always with him."

"Guess that's right. Way he asked about those three

hosses made me wonder. I bet he'd have left town if they'd been here.''

The girl's pretty face showed worry as she glanced at the top of the stairs. ''Grandpop, we have to get him out of town. Trying to make folk think he's Dusty Fog will get him killed. If Slingo Witch thinks he's Dusty Fog, he'll be after a fight. Even if that doesn't happen, one day the real Dusty Fog will catch up with him and do it.''

Pop nodded in agreement. ''Damned fool young button!'' he growled. ''He looks like a real nice kid.''

The ''fool young button,'' all unaware of the interest he was causing downstairs, and of the fate foreseen for him, finished shaving. He washed his face, dried it and dressed again, then swung his gun-belt on and went downstairs. He looked even younger now, shaved and washed, his hair combed tidily. Jean was reminded of a little boy, fresh tidied up and going to a party.

He followed them into the small dining-room and took the chair she indicated. Jean fetched in the food and served it out. She watched the two men eat, then took her own meal. She did not speak until they had finished the food and were drinking the coffee. Looking across the table she asked: ''Are you Dusty Fog?''

There was a slight pause. Then he nodded. ''Sure am.''

''Where are Mark Counter and the Ysabel Kid?'' she went on.

''We split up for a spell,'' the Texan replied, ignoring the breach of frontier good manners.

The girl glanced down at the table; she did not want to pry, but was trying to show the youngster that they knew he couldn't be Dusty Fog. ''Those aren't the guns you won at Tombstone, are they?''

The Texan shook his head; he noted the looks the girl was giving him. He'd seen that expression before, given by his own womenfolks. It meant: ''You aren't fooling me one little bit.''

Looking down at the tablecloth, to hide his grin, he answered, "Why no, they aren't. I don't tote them much at all."

For a long moment, Jean sat in silence, watching the young man. Then she said: "A man could get himself hurt, being called Dusty Fog."

The Texan looked back just as gravely, "Ma'am, you're so right about that. It happens most all the time."

The girl sighed; she'd hoped their guest would tell her the truth, and had even offered the olive branch to give him a chance to make his peace. She could go no further in the matter, without giving serious offence. Already she was well and beyond the bounds of frontier conversation.

"Will you be staying here for long?" she asked.

"Only until my amigos catch up with me. We aim to head down to Apache Country. Hear tell they're fixing in to hold a county fair, and I want to earn me some money."

"Shooting?"

"Trimming horses."

Pop looked up; he'd never heard of Dusty Fog trimming bad horses—even though he was known as a tophand at all branches of cattlework. "Got me a dun out there that needs trimming some."

Jean was wondering if the young man could pay for his room; but, before she could suggest that he worked for his keep, he solved the problem by taking money out and paying for a week. There was still a reasonable-sized roll left when he'd paid, and she decided he was the son of a well-to-do rancher who was travelling around for a holiday. That would account for his expensive hat and boots, and for his owning that magnificent stallion.

Pushing back his chair, the young man said, "I'll give him a whirl, if you like. I saw it in the corral; fair piece of hoss-flesh."

The two men left the house and Jean cleaned up then went out to watch them. The Texan had caught the dun and got it blindfolded; they were saddling it, and she watched him work. He knew horses very well, she could see that from the way in which he handled the dun, both during the saddling and after he got afork and removed the blindfold. The dun was only half-broken and went wild with rage at feeling a rider astride him again. The young Texan took the conceit out of that dun in big, solid chunks, and when he swung down, the horse knew that at least one man was his master.

"Like I said," the Texan remarked as he joined Pop outside the corral. "That's what a man'd call a fair piece of hoss-flesh. Got a whole heap of sand and he'll likely make a good sale."

"Will now he's been rid. But I never thought to get rid of him," Pop replied as he watched Jean return to the house. "Ain't had a hoss-buster since my son-in-law got killed. He could have handled this one, was going to start."

"He the one who's likeness is in my room?"

"Sure, Jack Mollison, as square a man as ever wore a badge."

"What happened to him?" the Texan asked. "If I'm talking too much, tell me so."

"He war shot down a week back. Gambling man called Barry Vent dropped him."

"Fair fight?"

"Dead fair." There was irony in Pop's tones. "That's the way it looked to all of us."

"This Barry Vent, he been round here long?" the Texan asked as he went into the corral and stripped the saddle from the subdued horse.

"Six months or so. Owns the Vent Bar, got a tough crowd at his back. One of them is Slingo Witch."

"Slingo Witch?" The Texan showed no great interest in the name. "They say he's fair with a gun."

"Fair?" Pop barked. Slingo Witch, for all his faults,

was a New Mexican. "Son, he's the fastest of them all."

"Do tell. The fastest I ever saw was a hand who rides for the Wedge. His name's Doc Leroy."

"He faster'n you?"

"He's the fastest I know."

It was with some misgivings that Jean watched the two men leave for the saloon as night came in. She hoped the young man would stay in the house, at least until she could talk him into leaving town. However, he insisted on going along with Pop and there was nothing she could do about it.

The saloon was well filled when they arrived; several cowhands from the local spreads were in, and the usual crowd of townsmen lounged around the bar. Pop Howard and the Texan came in. They halted and looked round. No one took any notice of them as they went to the bar. Johnny Sinclair and the thin old-timer who owned the post office and store, Edmund Ogilby, joined them. Pop introduced the youngster just as Dusty and left it at that; and neither thought anything of it. Pop decided that the boy was going to take their advice and stop pretending to be something he wasn't, and never could be—for he made no attempt to claim he was Dusty Fog.

They stood at the bar, talking, for a time, the saloon got noisier. Barry Vent arrived with Slingo Witch and the rest of his men. Benjy was there already; he was not sober and kept glaring sullenly at the blacksmith. At last, he rose and made an unsteady way across the room.

"Sinclair," he said. "I hear you've been talking real big about me and Jean Mollison."

Johnny came round, his hard-looking fists raising. "Keep her name out of it."

"Why?" Benjy sneered. "Just because you say so?"

"That's right."

Benjy grinned drunkenly and lifted his hands over the butts of his guns. He was standing well back and, even as drunk as he was, would have time to draw and put lead into the blacksmith before Sinclair could get to grips with him. He aimed to force the fight and down Sinclair before his brother, or Slingo Witch, could stop him. After that, they would have to back him up. He watched Johnny Sinclair and his hands moved slowly nearer to his guns.

"That's a powerful lot of force to use on a man without a gun."

Benjy took his eyes off Johnny Sinclair and stared at the small Texan. The man was facing Benjy now and his grey eyes met Benjy's without flickering. In that steady gaze, even a drunk could read trouble. Benjy looked down at the butt-forward guns. Confident that his brother's men would back him, he sneered:

"Now who asked you to stick your bill in, boy?"

"She's in, and in she stays," the young Texan replied, his voice still soft and easy; yet Pop noticed there was a subtle change in it.

"All right then." Benjy winked at Smith, behind the bar. "I'll take you. I handle men with guns."

The Texan looked him over in disgust. His voice was still low as he answered: "Make your play then—but, drunk or sober, I'll copper it."

The crowd watched, alert for trouble, some of the milder spirits taking cover in case shooting started. Smith reached under the bar for his shotgun and Pop Howard knew he must act fast or the young Texan would be killed.

"Hold it, Vent, afore you get hurt. This here is Dusty Fog."

Talk rolled up in a volume of sound as the words came to the crowd. There was not a man there who didn't know of the Rio Hondo gun-wizard. His mode of gun-toting was well-known; and the crowd wondered if this small man could really be the famous Dusty Fog.

Barry Vent and Slingo Witch looked at each other.

The gambler asked: "Is *that* him, Slingo?"

"Naw—he ain't wearing them gold-mounted guns. It ain't him."

Benjy Vent licked his lips. He saw, via the bar mirror's reflection, that the crowd seemed satisfied this man really was Dusty Fog. He didn't know if it was true or not; all he knew was that he didn't aim to try and find out. He missed the sign his brother passed to Smith and saw the man was polishing the bar-top, using both hands—which meant the shotgun was no longer backing him. He was scared, yet he did not want to back down.

Barry Vent pushed forward, between his brother and the Texan. Over his shoulder, he snapped: "Benjy you damned fool, get out of here before you get killed." Turning to the Texan he went on: "I'm sorry, Dusty. You know how these damned fool kids are when they've had a couple of drinks."

Benjy was about to open his mouth when a hand gripped his arm. He twisted round, muttering a curse which died as he looked at the impassive face of the hired killer. Slingo Witch forced him across the room and out of the door, then slapped him hard across the face, snarling: "Get home and stay there. If I see you again afore morning, I'll kill you."

Barry Vent waited until his brother had been evicted, then looked round at the crowd.

"Boys," he called, "we've got a chance to get us a lawman here at last. How about our asking Dusty if he'll take on the chore for us."

"Now wait a minute," Pop Howard put in. "Dusty ain't fixing to stay for but a few days. He don't——"

"Sure I'll take on," the Texan put in. "I need a riding chore, and this'll let me stay on here for a few days."

"All right then. That all fair with you boys?" Barry Vent yelled.

There was a shout of approval from the crowd, none of whom doubted any longer that this was Dusty Fog.

"Right, belly up to the bar then—drinks on the house!" Vent yelled.

In the crush to get the free drinks, the Texan found himself separated from Pop Howard. Barry Vent stood at his side. The gambler twisted round and looked at the small Texan, then in a low voice said: "Listen to me good, cowhand. I don't know who you are, only that you're not Dusty Fog. I run this town, and what I say goes. You forget that and I'll show you how the other Marshal died."

The young Texan looked down at Vent's gloved hands, then up at his face. "I remember real good, Mr. Vent. *Real* good."

Benjy Vent slammed into the chair by his brother's bed and snarled: "Why the hell did you do it? Taking that kid on as town badge."

Barry Vent looked up. He could read much the same question in the other faces, so decided to explain:

"We aim to pull a job right near this town. I don't want anybody here who might queer it. There's been talk of sending for John Poe, or Garrett, to handle the law here. Poe might do it, he's a friend of old Pop Howard. We don't want them in here."

"And with them thinking Dusty Fog is the law, they won't bother to come," Benjy put in.

"He's starting to think—I never knew he could," Barry scoffed. "We are only pulling off one more job, then we'll split up."

"Yeah, leave this one hoss town and head for the big cities," Benjy agreed. "But, before we go, I'm going to get Sinclair and that short-growed Texan both."

"Yeah, you do just that," Slingo Witch sneered. He knew that, whoever the small man was, even if he wasn't Dusty Fog, he was a good man with a gun. Slingo Witch could read the signs as well as any man; he

knew that the small Texan was in a far better class than
Benjy Vent—and, if Benjy went against him, there
would be a better share out of loot for the rest of the
Vent men.

"All right," Benjy sneered, looking round. "Comes
time for us to go. I'll get them both."

Another person was showing interest in the small
Texan. Jean Mollison looked at the star on his shirt as
they walked along behind the houses making for the
post office where she worked—trying to bring some
kind of solvency to a business which was owned by a
man with a thirst and a sadly wrong belief that there was
better than the 11-8 chance of filling an inside straight
on the draw.

"You're loco, Texas, that's what you are," she said,
refusing to be fooled into calling him Dusty Fog, even if
the rest of the town had fallen for it. "Do you know
what you've done?"

"Sure, took on a chore that'll bring me some money
in."

"But they made you marshal because they think
you're Dusty Fog. They won't like it when they find
out——" she paused, now knowing quite how to go on.

"That I'm not Dusty Fog?" he finished for her.
"Don't you think I am?"

The girl did not speak for a few moments; they were
coming near to the old cottonwood tree. She sighed and
shook her head. "You're a nice boy. But aren't you
taking this thing too far?"

"Maybe."

"When Barry Vent guesses you aren't Dusty Fog,
he'll send one of his men after you," she warned.

"He just might at that. But, when he does, I'll get
real worried."

"That he doesn't think you're Dusty Fog?"

"That he isn't sure if I am," the Texan answered.
"See, he already told me he knows I'm not."

Jean halted and faced the young man, hardly

knowing what to make of his soft-drawled words. They were under the spreading branches of the tree. She shuddered slightly, then said: "You may not know it, but this is where my father died."

"Sure—killed by Barry Vent."

Something in the way he said the words made her look hard at him, but she was unable to read a thing from his face. "By Barry Vent—and you may be next."

"Who saw the shooting?"

"No one I know of. Gramps was out back, but all he heard was the shot. When he turned, it was all over."

The Texan was looking at the tree. He turned and looked at the gap between the two houses and the building across the street. He turned back to the girl once again.

"Was it a fair fight?"

"They must have drawn against each other, and Dad got off one shot." Jean fought down rising grief, guessing that the young man was not just making small talk, nor satisfying idle curiosity.

"Where was your pappy stood, under the tree, with Vent across there, back to the alley?" The girl nodded, and he went on: "And how tall was your pappy?"

"Six foot odd."

The Texan turned his attention to the tree again. He took out a knife and opened the blade, then started to cut into the bark of the tree. He worked carefully, gouging into the trunk. Finally, he dug out a battered piece of lead, which he juggled up and down in his palm.

"No witnesses; nobody real near. Only one shot, or sounded like that."

Jean stared at the young man for a moment before the meaning of the words hit her. "How did you know the shots were so close together that they sounded like one?"

"Just guessed. See, I know a man called Sam Bass and he told me about some gambler called Vent."

"Sam Bass—you mean the outlaw?"

"Ain't more than one of them, I reckon," he replied, a grin playing on his lips. "I know Sam—not in the line of duty, as you might say, but well enough. Met him up to Bent's Ford last time and we got to talking about this and that. He told me about a man called Barry Vent."

Her eyes were on his face; there was far more to this small man than first met the eye. "What do you mean about Barry Vent?"

"Who owns a set of gold scales in town?" He ignored her last question.

"We have a set of gold scales up at the store. Come along and Mr. Ogilby will let you use them."

They walked on to the post office and entered together. Ogilby looked up, his pallid face working nervously. He came forward, laying aside his broom when he saw the Texan.

"Howdy, Marshal. What can I do for you?"

"Like to use your gold scales, if you don't mind."

"Sure." Ogilby waved a hand to the glass-covered, delicately-balanced scales on the counter before him. "Bought them when I thought I'd light out for the Black Hills, but I never got a chance. Only time they get used now is when some old prospector comes in with some dust."

The Texan removed the glass cover and bent over the scales. Jean watched him for a moment, then went behind the counter to start work. If she had stayed, the young man's actions might have given her cause to worry about his welfare even more.

First, he put the battered piece of lead on the scales. Then, taking a .45 bullet from his belt-loops, he pried the head off and dropped it on the other scale. He touched the lever and the battered piece of lead sank down. He nodded and removed the .45, then asked: "Do you sell either Winchester .45, .75, or Sharps .50 shells?"

"Only Sharps, never get no call for them new model Winchester bullets yet," Ogilby replied.

"I'd like one Sharps bullet."

"Only one?"

"Figger that'd be enough."

Ogilby crossed the room and, from an open box, took a single, long Sharps rifle bullet. He handed this to the Texan, who removed the head as he had with the .45 then set it on the scales. He took the battered piece of lead off the other pan, replacing it with the .45. The Sharps bullet head dragged the scales down as had the other. He removed the .45 bullet head and replaced it with the piece of lead. This time the balance was made, the scales remaining level.

"Like an envelope," the Texan said.

Jean brought him the envelope. He put the three pieces of lead into it, sealed the flap then asked them both to sign their names over the seal. Both did as they were asked, seething with questions; but something in his face stopped them from asking.

"Who owns a Sharps round here?"

"Johnny Sinclair, Pop Howard, several of the ranchers, Slingo Witch, a few more," Ogilby replied.

The Texan pushed the envelope into his pocket, then looked them over; somehow, he looked older now. "I'd take it kind if neither of you said anything about what I've been doing."

The door swung closed behind the Texan. The man and the girl looked at each other. It was some seconds before either spoke. Ogilby licked his lips, then asked: "What do you make of that?"

"I don't know, but that boy is going to get himself in bad trouble before he's through here."

Ogilby shook his head, he kept his thoughts to himself. They, like Jean's, were on the small man, but they were very different.

The Texan walked along the street. He was about to

go into the jail when he saw a woman coming from the house which faced the cottonwood. He crossed the street and met her, removing his hat.

"Howdy ma'am. Do you let out your rooms?"

She stopped, looking him over for a moment, then shook her head. "I do, but I don't have any to spare now. Mr. Vent took them all. I'm working out all day, and they take care of themselves."

"Thank you ma'am. I'll just stay on with the Howards for a spell. You say you're away from home all day?"

"Yes, every day—down at the Eating House."

The Texan turned back and crossed to the jail. He opened the door and looked at the office. It was still as when Jack Mollison left it, the table dusty and the report-book still lying open on the desk. He crossed the room, checking on the two cells at the back, then opened the safe with the keys Pop Howard had turned over to him that morning. He tossed the envelope inside and was about to close the door when he saw the wig. Taking it out, he turned it over in his hands, then tossed it back and went to sit at the desk, glancing down at the report-book. He read the open page, rose and went to the safe again, taking out the wig and looked it over once more. Finally, he tossed it back into the safe and locked the door again.

Returning to the desk, he read through the report on the Shotgun Gang more carefully. He was still reading when the door of the office was thrown open and a man looked in. He'd been running, and gasped: "Marshal, Benjy Vent and three of his brother's men are beating Johnny Sinclair up."

The Texan's chair slid back and he left the office fast, heading for the blacksmith's shop at a dead run. The other man came at a more leisurely pace, wanting to see if this lawman would dare to tangle with Barry Vent's men. There had been some sober thought about the small man since the previous night, and few of the men who'd seen the Texan now really believed that he was Dusty Fog at all.

The Texan turned the corner and went round to the forge. He saw the man was speaking the truth. Johnny Sinclair had put up quite a fight and all the Vent men were marked by his hard fists. Haines was leaning against the wall, holding his jaw, Brandon and Wheeler were holding the blacksmith; and Benjy Vent picked up a hammer, coming forward.

"I'm going to fix you real good, big man," he snarled.

He swung up the hammer and, at the same moment, Brandon yelled a warning. A hand gripped Benjy's shoulder, spinning him round. He saw the small Texan in front of him. Then a fist smashed into his stomach, doubling him in agony. The Texan sent another punch on the tail of the first, catching Benjy's jaw as it came down. For one so small, the Texan could hit. Benjy Vent looked as if he were trying to go two ways at once. The hammer fell from his hand, and he went down hard on to his back.

Brandon released Sinclair's arm and hurled at the small Texan. The lanky man appeared to knock the other clean off his feet, but there was a slight difference. The Texan was going over backwards, even before Brandon reached him. Two hands gripping at Brandon's vest, pulling him forward. A foot rammed into his stomach and, the next instant, the world seemed to spin round. He smashed down on to the ground, flat on his back.

Haines came back from the wall, his foot lashing back into the Texan's ribs. He rolled over and, as Haines came in for another kick, got a foot behind the man's ankle, put his other on the knee—and shoved. With one foot off the ground, Haines was thrown clean off-balance and joined his pard in the dirt. The Texan came up in a lithe bound and watched Johnny Sinclair

throw Wheeler from him. The man hit the wall and
came off again. Sinclair's fist shot out, smashing into
his face. Wheeler went over backwards, his head
crashed into the wall and he went down to lay still. Then
Johnny yelled a warning, for Haines was pulling a knife
as he came at the Texan.

The small young man moved faster than Sinclair had
ever seen: he weaved under a slash of the knife and came
up with his hand lashing round. He struck in a way
which was new to the blacksmith. Instead of clenching
his whole fist he only closed his second, third and fourth
fingers, holding the forefinger and thumb bent slightly
crooked. His arm drove out, the finger and thumb
catching Haines in the throat on either side of the
Adam's apple. He gave a croaking cry and his face
turned a shade of greyish green as he stumbled backwards. The Texan's other hand came round, this time
with the fingers rigid and the thumb bent. The base of
the hand caught the other man at the side of the neck.
He went down, flopping like a back-broke rabbit.

Brandon caught up a pitchfork, gripping it in his
hands as he came at the small man. The Texan went forward, one arm going up to cover his head as he dived
over, rolling right under the fork and into Brandon's
feet. The man yelled as he went over, crashing into the
wall. He came up and saw the Texan was already on his
feet. Brandon howled in fury and charged wildly forward. The Texan avoided the wild and clumsy blows.
His fist drove out this time, the forefinger bent and
extended ahead of the others. Brandon's head jerked.
The blow landed just under his bottom lip and, with
red, roaring pain filling him, he went down.

It was then that Benjy Vent tried to take a hand. He
started to sit up and his right hand dropped towards the
gun in his belt. Sinclair yelled in fury and leapt on the
dandy, crushing him to the ground. Two huge hands
closed on Benjy's throat, squeezing hard, lifting his
head to smash it on to the ground.

The Texan looked around; quite a crowd was gathered staring at the three men laying on the ground. Then he saw Slingo Witch, Smith and Barry Vent coming towards the forge. He gave his attention to the blacksmith—who was still on top of Benjy Vent, choking him until his face was turning purple and he was croaking in agony.

"Loose off, Johnny!" he snapped. "Let loose— before you kill him."

Sinclair did not let loose; he was in that slow-burning, yet deadly, rage which comes when an even-tempered man is pushed too far. The Texan knew that, unless Johnny Sinclair had let loose by the time Vent arrived, he would die. Stepping forward, the Texan swung his hand again, the fingers extended. The edge of the hand drove into Sinclair's arm, sending agony knifing through it and causing it to loose its grip.

"What the hell?" he asked, staring dazedly up at the Texan.

"I had to stop you before you finished him off," was the reply. "Get up."

Sinclair got to his feet, rubbing his numb arm and trying to work his fingers to get use back into them. "How did you do it, and where did you learn to hit like that?"

"I'll tell you some time," the Texan answered, picking up the guns which had fallen from his holsters. He checked them over and slipped them back to leather again.

Barry Vent came through the crowd, his two men flanking him. They all halted, and looked down at the forms on the ground. Barry Vent's eyes went from one of his men to the others and halted on his brother. Then he looked at Johnny Sinclair, who was standing up near to the anvil. Finally, he turned his gaze to the small Texan, and asked:

"What's all this about?"

"Your boys got themselves all tuckered out."

Vent scowled at the small man, detecting the hidden mockery in the tones. "That's my brother. What did you do to him?"

"Nothing to what he and your men were fixing in to do to Johnny there," the Texan replied. "Mister, they were ganged up four against one—and I don't stand for that, any time."

Vent stiffened. Slingo Witch watched the Texan with fresh interest. Smith wondered if they were making a mistake and selling this small, insignificant-looking man short.

"I don't like what you've done here!" Vent began.

"Mister, I don't care. Like Sam Bass once told me——"

"Sam Bass?" Vent lost his poker face for a moment. "Do you know Sam Bass?"

"Some, heard him sing baritone in a quartet with one of my amigos, Chris Madsen and Bent from Bent's Ford," the Texan answered.

For a moment Vent was silent; he'd heard the Texas outlaw, Sam Bass, talk of singing in a quarter with U.S. Marshal Chris Madsen and two other men. This Texan must know Bass well—and any man who knew Bass was a serious danger to Barry Vent's safety.

The air was suddenly charged with danger, the crowd scattering back as Barry Vent nodded to his men. They moved out from him slightly, watching the Texan, and knowing that they were up against a man at least as good as themselves. The Texan watched them, his hands held slightly in front of his body, the fingers slightly bent, ready to make his move.

"Mr. Vent! Mr. Vent!" Ogilby pushed through the crowd. "I got a telegraph message for you. It looks important."

Vent took the form from the old man's hand, opened it and read: "Cargo of whisky on next delivery. Sorry short notice." There was no return address or name of sender.

"Leave it for now," he said softly. "Get the boys back to the saloon, Slingo."

The Texan jerked his head and ordered several men to help tote the unconscious men away. He watched Vent and the two hired killers walking away and frowned, wondering what was in the message that it had brought such a change in Vent. Johnny Sinclair let out his breath in a long, slow blow, lowering the hammer he held back to the anvil.

"I've seen it all now. I surely thought they meant to draw on you."

The Texan grinned. "You figure on knocking the bullet back at them?"

"I figgered to split Slingo Witch's skull if he killed you."

Jean arrived at a dead run, thrusting through the crowd and flinging her arms round Johnny's neck, gasping: "Johnny you're all right?"

"Sure," Sinclair answered blushing furiously. "Texas here helped a lot. I've never seen a man fight like he can. He licked that bunch himself."

The girl stared at the small man, fear in her eyes. "Now you've done it. Barry Vent will send his men after you, and they'll get you. Aren't you worried?"

"I will be when he sends them after me, like I told you. I wonder what that telegraph message was about."

"Telegraph message?" Jean frowned. "I haven't seen one all day. I did see Mr. Ogilby writing on a blank form——"

The Texan nodded; now he could see it. Ogilby knew something about Barry Vent; that message proved it. There would be questions to be asked, and Ogilby was one of the men who knew the answers. Barry Vent was suspicious; he would be more so now he knew this small man knew Sam Bass. Things were going to happen faster than the Texan wanted in Tensonville.

"Is he Dusty Fog?"

Barry Vent looked at his boss trigger-man, on the evening after the fight. They were in the saloon; no customers were here as yet, and they were talking in soft tones—which would not carry to the ears of the other members of the Vent bunch, who were drinking at the far end of the bar.

The killer shook his head. "I don't know, Barry, and that's the truth. I could go and find out."

Barry Vent was considering making the same suggestion, but prudence was prevalent and he decided against it. Slingo Witch was very fast; but, if this man should be Dusty Fog, the killer wouldn't be fast enough. Vent thought of the money in his safe and the plans he had for it. Slingo Witch was indispensable for those plans.

"No. One of the others might be better," he answered.

"Benjy?" Witch asked mockingly.

Barry Vent shook his head as if he took the suggestion seriously. "Not this time. We may need him when the time comes to share out."

"Which won't be long now."

"No, the coach will be coming through tomorrow. We'll take it five miles out of town, come back and clean up here, then get clear."

Shorty Smith came along the bar, watching the other two and wondering what they were discussing. He jerked a thumb to where the other men were standing and drinking. "You'd best talk to Brandon. He aims to kill that Texan."

Vent nodded. "I thought he might. I'll try and stop him."

Brandon was standing at the bar, teetering on his heels, and looking in the glassy-eyed way a bad, mean drunk showed. He looked at the others for a moment, then snarled: "I'm going to kill that damned runt."

Barry Vent came along the bar, laying his hand on the

other's arm. Brandon swung round but the ugly snarl changed to a slobbering grin as he recognised his boss.

"You tell 'em, boss. I c'n kill that runt, can't I?"

"Sure, Sam, sure. Nobody allows you're scared of him at all."

Brandon stared owlishly at Vent, from the tone his boss used, someone had said he was scared. He teetered on his heels again and glared round at the others, yelling: "Who said I was scared of him?"

"None of us, Sam." Again Vent managed to sound as if the word had been said.

"Well, I ain't scared of him. Ain't scared of nobody, I ain't. I'll show you. Where is he?"

Smith looked from the window; the Texan was walking along the street with Pop Howard and Sinclair. "He's out there on Main Street right now."

"Now then, Sam," Vent put in. "We're your friends, so you don't have to prove anything to us. We know you can lick him."

"That's right, Barry. I c'n lick him. And I'm *going* to," Brandon replied. He pushed from the bar and glared belligerently. "Don't none of you try and stop me. I'm going to kill me a man."

Not one of the others tried to stop Brandon for two reasons: one was that they knew he was dead mean when in likker; the other was that, if he died, their own share in the loot would be greater. They watched him cross the room, and few of them doubted that he would walk back.

"I tried to stop him," Barry Vent remarked. "The damned fool."

"Hope he comes back again," Smith answered—in a tone which showed he hoped no such thing and held even less than hope if he did mean it.

The Texan walked along the street with Howard and Sinclair, talking of range matters. He paid little attention to the man who came from the Vent Bar, apart from noticing that he appeared drunk. He carried on with his description of how to "goodnight" a bull, until Brandon yelled: "Texas!" he screeched, "I'm coming for you."

"Stand clear, and keep out of it," the Texan snapped to the other two. "I can handle it."

Howard and Sinclair pulled aside, to the edge of the street. The Texan stayed where he was, hands hanging by his sides, eyes never leaving the other man. Brandon advanced, swaying slightly yet steadying as the cold air brought him more to his senses. Suddenly, the man realised that he was involved in something far worse than usual. He'd expected, in his drunken way, that the mere sight of himself primed for war and pawing dirt would be enough to scare this small man away. Yet the Texan showed no sign of fear or flinching; he just stood there without moving, those grey eyes never leaving Brandon's face.

"Going to kill you!" his words were not so wild, not certain now; but he would not back down.

"Go to bed and sleep it off." The Texan did not raise his voice.

"Draw!" Brandon screamed back.

"Not until you do. But, if you go for your gun, I'll kill you. Drunk or sober, I'll kill you."

Brandon licked his lips; he was afraid of this small man. But it wasn't a small man standing there now. It was a big man, a man who stood larger than any other Brandon had ever seen. Then pride stopped Brandon from turning and running. This was not Dusty Fog. It was only a fool kid acting like him.

His hand went down, gripping the butt of the gun.

The Texan's right hand twisted, palm out, and the white-handled gun came from leather in a fast-done twist-hand draw. It slid clear and the side of his forearm pressed tighter than was usual against his body. The left hand came across, the heel of it catching the hammer

spur to force it back, lifted and made a circle to repeat
the cocking as the balance of the Colt settled it in line
once more. The two shots sounded so close together that
they were barely two separate noises. Brandon rocked
back on his heels, his gun clear of leather. The striking
power of two bullets coming so close together threw him
backwards from his feet, his own shot going wide. The
Texan advanced and looked down at Brandon, then
holstered his gun again.

In the saloon, Vent's bunch stared out of the window. For a time none of them spoke. Then Barry Vent
laughed—a savage cough of laughter.

"He's not Dusty Fog. Way I heard it, Dusty Fog pulls
crossdraw. Besides, he fanned the hammer—and no
good man does that."

Slingo Witch was silent; he only partly agreed with
Vent. True, Dusty Fog used the cross-draw, not the
cavalry twist; but Vent was wrong on the other thing.
Fanning was used by only two kind of people: greeners
trying to show off, and the very best men with a gun.
Only one of the best men would gamble his life on so
risky a trick; and, the way the Texan handled his gun, he
was no greener.

"It ain't Dusty Fog—but he's still good with a gun,"
he replied.

The killing of Brandon set the whole town talking; there
was no other subject of conversation. Arguments waved
hotly as men argued that the small Texan was, or was
not, Dusty Fog. The main argument was about the manner in which the Texan drew when he killed Brandon,
for Dusty Fog was known to draw across his body. It
was generally conceded that, although the youngster
might be better than fair with a gun, he was not Dusty
Fog; and that was how matters stood the following
morning.

"Why don't you get out of town, boy?" Jean

Mollison looked gravely at her guest the following morning as he finished his breakfast. "The others will be coming after you."

"No, I don't think so, I bought me some more time last night."

Pop looked at the Texan too, then remarked: "Way I heard it, Dusty Fog uses the cross-draw."

"Do tell." The Texan's face held a smile which was both mocking and friendly. "Happen you were in the cavalry? Well, they tote their guns like this, so they can get at the gun with either hand. I wear mine for the same reason, so I can get at either gun with either hand."

"Show me your draw, please," Jean put in.

"What would it prove?" he replied. "Knew a man one time who was always making what looked like real fast draws. Had a lot of folks scared of him—until he went and got killed in a gun-fight with a boy he didn't scare. Thing was, the boy wasn't fast who beat him."

"Then you won't run?" she asked.

"Nope. I'm still waiting for my friends."

Pop snorted angrily and slapped a hand on the table. "We'll put that on your tombstone."

"Why, thank you most to death," the Texan answered as he hand-rolled a smoke.

The Texan spent the day around town; he watched Barry Vent, Slingo Witch, Haines and Wheeler leave, and trailed them for a couple of miles. Then he returned to Tensonville again. He stayed in the jail office, reading through the report on the Shotgun Gang, for a time. Then he took the wig from the safe again. Night was falling, and he sat there staring down at the red hair. Then he pushed back his chair, took out his guns, checked the loads and left the room.

Benjy Vent was drunker than usual. He stood at the bar and looked round the room, then at Smith behind the bar. "Look at 'em, Smith," he said, waving a hand to the men who were at the tables. "All these bunch here. Don't they make you want to retch?"

Smith scowled at the young man; Benjy was talking too much and would need shutting up soon. The bar-dog moved along and growled. "You'd best get to bed, boy. You know what Barry's told you about shooting off your mouth?"

"Why worry, Smith? After tomorrow, we won't need this town no more—and we'll be long gone. Us, and that you-know-what in the safe."

"Shut up!" Smith bellowed.

"Why should I?" Benjy twisted round. " 'Cause you tell me to? Won't need you bunch after today. I'm going to talk if I want."

Smith scowled, looking at Benjy Vent through slitted eyes. His suspicions were being confirmed; the Vent brothers and Slingo Witch were planning to double-cross the others. This drunken young fool was talking too much though. No one in town knew what Vent and his men were doing here, and it would be better if they never found out.

Benjy Vent leered round; he was staggering along the bar and forgetting that Smith was watching him with suspicious gaze. He stopped and stared at Pop Howard and Ogilby, who were playing crib at a table.

"Know what we want in this place, Shorty?" he asked, swaying towards the small bartender confidentially. "We wants a gal here to liven things up. So I'm going to fetch Jean Mollison here."

Pop's chair scraped back as he came to his feet. "You drunken no-good!" he hissed. "Leave my gal's name out of it?"

"Yeah?" Benjy sneered. "Why? Just 'cause you say so? You just fill your hand if you reckon you can stop me."

Pop gulped; he was not wearing a gun, as just coming to the saloon did not seem to call for it. All too well, he knew that Benjy Vent would kill him the more willingly as he was helpless. He held his hands from his sides and said: "I don't have a gun."

"You drunken, no-good little rat!"

Benjy Vent rocked back on his heels as if he'd been hit. He stared with unbelieving eyes at old Ogilby—who was standing up now, his thin old face hard and filled with loathing. The old man's hands shook as he faced this bullying youth who'd made his life miserable for so long.

"What did you say?" Benjy gasped.

"You damned drunken hawg," Ogilby answered. "You think you're so smart. I've known all along what you and your brother've been doing here in town. And I know they won't find any stage-coach. I sent that message he got to stop them killing Johnny Sinclair and the Texan."

Smith started to snarl and curse, but Benjy was white with rage and screamed: "You old——"

The gun came out without Benjy even knowing it, hammer tearing back and throwing lead into Ogilby's thin frame. The old man rocked backwards off his feet and crashed to the ground. Pop Howard dropped to his knees beside his friend; he looked down at Ogilby's face, amazed at the relaxed, satisfied look on it. Then he looked up at Benjy Vent, who had holstered the gun again and was grinning mirthlessly and drunkenly down.

"You won't get away with this. I'll see you hang for it."

"Will you now?" Benjy jeered. "Well——"

"I'll take your guns!"

The words, soft and drawling though they were, cut through the air like a whip and sounded clear across the room.

Benjy Vent turned and stared at the bat-wing doors, and the small Texan who stood just inside them. Yet it was not the same man who stood there. He looked older, cold, deadly and dangerous.

"Get out of here!" Benjy snarled.

The Texan advanced across the room. There was

something deadly, latently savage about him, but Benjy's drink dulled mind did not see it. Behind the bar, Smith saw it. He saw it and recognized it for what it was. Seeing it, he moved along, hand falling to the butt of his sawed-off shotgun under the bar. He was a gun-fighting man, but knew that here was his master in a straight grab and shoot. The scatter-gun was his best bet now, if Benjy held the Texan's attention.

"Shed that belt," the Texan told Benjy.

"Boy, you're letting that badge go to your head. I know you ain't Dusty Fog."

"Get it off!" It was not a polite request now but an order.

Benjy Vent sent his right hand down towards his gun-butt, and, behind the bar, Smith started to bring his shotgun out. The Texan's hands crossed in a flickering, sight-defying blur of movement. The bar-light caught and threw back a dull flicker from the blued barrels of the matched guns as they came out, flame tearing from the muzzle. Benjy Vent rocked back on to his heels as lead smashed into his shoulder. He hit the bar and went down, screaming in pain, his gun falling from his hand. At the same instant, Smith was hurled back into the wall, bringing some bottles down from the shelf. For an instant he stood erect, but the hole between his eyes showed that it was only the muscular reaction of a dead man.

Even as Smith's body fell to the ground, the Texan moved forward. He flipped the right-hand gun back to leather and bent over to remove Vent's second gun. Then he looked up at Pop Howard. "Get him down to the jail. Is Mr. Ogilby dead?"

Pop nodded. He looked at the guns, then at the small man, "He's dead. That lousy rat there——"

"Take him to jail," the Texan repeated softly.

"Sure, where's Barry Vent and Slingo Witch?"

"Left town this morning. I followed them for a couple of miles."

"Then you'd better get out too, Dusty." For the first time, Pop had no doubts as to the small man's identity.

"Not yet. There's something more than meets the eye here, and I aim to stay and see what it is. One thing, I know for sure: Barry Vent never killed your son-in-law."

"What do you mean?"

"I can't explain now. But I want Benjy Vent down at the jail."

Pop dragged the young man to his feet, ignoring any pain he might be causing. He pushed Benjy Vent towards the door, bent and picked up one of the youngster's guns, and followed him out. The Texan looked round at the crowd, then called two of the town businessmen over, telling them to check the cash-desk and put all the money in a sack. Two more men were given the task of carrying Smith's body to the undertaker's shop. The rest were told that the saloon was closed for the night, and there was no argument. Not one man here was sure if this was really Dusty Fog or not, but they were not going to argue with him.

The saloon was closed when Pop Howard came back from the jail. The Texan stood on the porch, a small, insignificant figure among the tall men who were on the street. Yet, for all of that, Pop went to him—for, inside there, he'd been taller than them all.

"You're Dusty Fog, aren't you?" he asked.

"Your gal doesn't reckon so," the Texan replied. "Come up to the jail with me again. I want something doing."

Pop walked back along the street with the Texan, listening to the soft-spoken orders; in spite of his grief at losing an old friend, he managed a chuckle at the end and said: "It'll work."

"Sure. But you see that they know they're doing it for my end. If they try to do it for their own, I'll stop them."

Benjy Vent lay on the bed in the cell. The town doctor

had fixed his wound and he was alone. His eyes were no longer drunk as he looked up at the small Texan. "You'll get your'n!" he snarled.

"Likely. Happen you won't be round to see it though."

"What do you mean?" Benjy Vent heard shouting and an angry roaring from down by the saloon.

"Folks'll take any amount of abuse, but there comes a breaking point. You reached it when you gunned down old Ogilby. They liked him—and they don't like you."

Then Benjy Vent heard the shouts drawing closer; he could make out what they were saying. He felt sudden, cold deep fear at the words, and the angry tones of the crowd as they came nearer: "Lynch him! Get a rope!"

"It's bad, Vent. They want to hang you." The Texan turned on his heel, to walk towards the door.

"Where you going?" Benjy screamed.

"Me? To bed. If I stay here, I'll have to stop them—and I surely don't aim to kill decent folks to save you."

"You got to save me—you're the law!"

The Texan shrugged. "Your brother told me that he was the law. He might come back in time to save you."

"I'll tell you where he is!" Benjy Vent gasped. "He's out robbing a stage. He's the leader of the Shotgun Gang."

The Texan stopped. A rock hit the door of the jail and outside, the yells grew louder. He ignored the sounds and went to the desk, opened it and took out a sheet of paper and a pen. Sitting down, he started to write—and Benjy Vent talked:

"Barry got this bunch together; him and Slingo Witch. They picked four men who looked alike. When we went out on a hold-up Smith and Wheeler stopped in town and took turns as barman and waiter. Smith dressed like Haines when he was acting as a waiter, and wore a red wig. Nobody ever cottoned on; they didn't know us well enough to notice any difference. Worked the same with Brandon and Wheeler. Then I lost the wig, and Mollison found it. Barry knew he was suspicious, so we had to get rid of him.''

"So you shot him with that Sharps as he drew on your brother?''

"Not me. Slingo Witch did it——'' Benjy began. Then his mouth dropped open, and he stared at the small man. "How'd you know that?''

"I know it. Get on—who's your contact man in Wells Fargo?''

Benjy talked, long, loud and eagerly, laying bare his brother's secrets in his terrified bid to prevent the crowd from getting at him. He was pathetically eager to help this small man—who, only a short time before, he'd been ready to kill. The Texan ignored the noise outside, the pen in his left hand moving over the paper fast as he took down the story.

The door of the jail opened. The Texan came round fast, the pen falling to the desk as his left-hand gun came out and lined. Benjy Vent gave a scream of fear and cowered back in his cell as Pop Howard and another man came in, lifting their hands shoulder high.

"Easy boy, easy!'' Pop yelled.

"All right.'' The gun went back and the Texan took up the pen with his right hand.

Benjy Vent stared at the two men, yelling for the Texan to stop them getting at him. He backed into the far corner and cowered down as the small man came to the door, carrying the sheet of paper.

"Did you tell me all that's on this paper?'' he asked.

"Sure, sure I did!'' Benjy half-screamed back. "Don't let them touch me!''

Pop Howard snapped: "Look at that yeller rat. He's not so high and mighty now.''

The Texan opened the cell and went inside. He rested the confession on his knee and held out the pen to Benjy Vent, saying: "Make your mark with your good hand.'' Then, after the mark was made, he left the cell and told Pop to witness the other's signature. "You too, friend."

After the second man signed, the Texan took the paper to the desk and added his own signature. Without letting the others see it, he folded the sheet and sealed it in an envelope.

"Tell the boys to go home now," he said to Pop. "I want you to stay here all night, if you will."

Barry Vent and his men rode into town shortly after dawn on the morning after the shooting. They came along main street, riding in a bunch. There were ugly expressions on their faces as they made for the Vent Bar.

The Texan watched them go by. Then he checked the loads of his matched guns and pulled his hat on, then stepped out. Jean caught his arm.

"Don't go down there!" she gasped. "Please don't go down there. Let Gramps get the men of the town together."

"Nope, the town hired me as their law. I won't stack them against guns to do my work. Besides, I'll have the edge, if I get to them first."

Jean watched the small man walk away towards the Vent Bar. Her face was pale as she imagined the scene at the saloon, that small man stacking up against the deadly killer, Slingo Witch. Then, from in front of the house, she heard the sound of hooves and four men rode by. She glanced at them idly. Then her eyes widened and she gasped: "No. It *can't* be. It can't!" Jean ran round the side of the house as the four strangers turned their mounts to head for the corral.

"I'm with you, Marshall!"

Johnny Sinclair stepped from the sidewalk as the Texan made his way towards the saloon. The blacksmith held a shotgun under his arm and swung alongside the small young man.

"No. I can handle it, Johnny."

"Not alone, you don't."

They stepped on to the sidewalk and across. Side-by-side they pushed open the bat-wings and entered. Barry Vent twisted round, his face unshaven, hard and angry.

"What do you want?" he asked.

"You. I'm arresting you on a charge of hold-up and murder."

Vent's men fanned out, the killer, Slingo Witch, standing at his boss's right, big, deadly looking and ready. The other two moved to get a clear line of fire. Barry Vent asked: "Where's Benjy and Smith?"

"I killed Smith and jailed your brother," the Texan replied. "He talked real loud and long."

"Get him!" Barry Vent hissed.

"Just try it," the Texan answered.

Barry Vent watched the small Texan, noting those matched, butt-forward guns, the well-made buscadero belt, the easy, relaxed confidence of the young man. He felt scared, knowing that he'd made a terrible mistake.

"There's four of us against you," he warned.

"Sure, but figure it this way: happen I'm Dusty Fog, how many of you will live to touch leather?"

"Me!"

Slingo Witch snarled, his hands lashing down to the butts of his guns.

Flame tore from the muzzles of the Texan's guns, the two shots sounding as one. Slingo Witch was lifted clear from his feet by the smashing impact of the two bullets, his own weapons falling from his hands. The Texan's guns went back to leather once more. In that brief instant, before any other man in the room could move, it was all over. Slingo Witch lay dead, and the Texan's guns were back in their holsters again. It was gun-work of a savage and terrible nature.

Barry Vent looked at the other two men, all knowing that the only way they could get away from here was to kill the Texan. Johnny Sinclair did not even enter into their calculations. Haines licked his lips; he'd been in prison before, and the thought of it scared him.

"Well?" the Texan asked.

Barry Vent jerked his head to the other two; he still could not believe the Texan was Dusty Fog, and was willing to gamble. Then he heard boot-heels thud and the bat-wing doors swung open. Four tall Texas cowhands came in, fanning out into a half-circle behind the small man.

"Dusty, you surely lost the bet," the handsome blond giant at the left said.

Barry Vent slumped; he knew all was up now. No two men could stand up to that quartet, even if the other wasn't——

"You're Dusty Fog, aren't you?" he asked hoarsely.

"Didn't you know, mister?" the tall, wide-shouldered youngster at the other side of the group asked.

"Waco!" the small Texan snapped. "Get the guns from those two. Leave the gambler's."

The youngster moved forward; but he moved as a trained lawman, keeping well clear of the line of fire. The other three, the handsome blond giant, the black-dressed, baby-faced boy with the butt-forward old Dragoon gun, and the freckle-faced red-head, stood relaxed, yet ready for action.

"Jail's along the street there, Mark. Take these two down, Waco, Red, go with him. Lon, this here's Mr. Barry Vent."

The men left and Vent stood looking at the three who remained. He looked at the small man called Dusty Fog; then at the black-dressed youngster known as the Ysabel Kid; then at Johnny Sinclair.

Dusty took out his right-hand gun and pushed it into Johnny Sinclair's waistband, taking the shotgun. Then he stepped back and said:

"Johnny, this is the man who shot down your Marshal. I want you to take him. He's all yours."

Johnny looked down at the gun; he was a poor performer with a six-gun and not trained for such things. Then he saw sweat running down Vent's face and said:

"All right, you've got your choice. Pull it, or give up."

Barry Vent's hand jerked spasmodically, the fingers working; but he made no attempt to draw. Slowly, he dropped his left hand to the belt-buckle and unfastened it. The gunbelt fell to his feet. He stumbled forward, past the other men, making for the door. Dusty caught his arm, turned him and pulled the glove from his right hand. Johnny Sinclair looked closer; the hand was badly scarred and marked.

"I didn't kill Mollison. It was Slingo Witch, with his Sharps," Vent said. "How did you know?"

"When you met Sam Bass, and tried to get him interested in this idea of yours. Benjy got drunk. He told him all about how you had a gun-bust in your hand and daren't touch one since. I knew from the start that, if you were the Barry Vent Sam told me about, you couldn't have shot the Marshal. So I dug the bullet from the tree, it weighed nearer a Sharp's fifty than a forty-five."

Johnny Sinclair picked up the fallen gun-belt and removed the gun from its holster. The metal work inside the holster was rusted, and the gun was not loaded. "What's it all about?"

"Vent ran the Shotgun Gang. I've got the full story at the jail. Come down and read it."

Jean Mollison and her grandfather looked at the group around the table. The young woman shook her head as Dusty Fog hand-rolled a smoke, and said: "You never believed I was me, if you follow me."

"And you know why," she replied.

"Sure, I don't wear those two gold-mounted guns I won at Tombstone. They're Cavalry model, and don't balance like these old Civilian model plowhandles."

"You surely had us all fooled," Pop put in. "I wasn't sure who you was until you downed Smith."

Dusty did not reflect the grins on the other four faces. "It cost Brandon his life. If I'd drawn cross-hand I'd

have been able to just cripple him. With the twist-hand
draw, I had to shoot to kill. I didn't want trouble and I
had to make Vent sure I wasn't Dusty Fog. It bought me
another day or so.''

"And, when you came here to ask about the paint, I
thought you were scared the real Dusty Fog was here,"
Jean told him.

"Sure. See, we made a bet that we could separate for
a month and get here without getting into trouble, so I
tried to avoid trouble. I asked to see if any of the others
were here."

"You just lay your money on the table, Cap'n Fog,"
the Ysabel Kid remarked.

"Why sure," Dusty agreed, laying thirty dollars on
the table. "How'd you get on, Waco?"

"Reckon a man'd say I lost, too," Waco replied.

CHAPTER TWO

A Second Case of Mistaken Identity

"Bill! Bill Longley!"

Waco brought his big paint stallion to a halt as a well-dressed old-timer stepped from the sidewalk and came towards him, beaming with delight. The young man looked round to see if the notorious gentleman from Mill Creek, Texas, was riding behind him. But the street was clear; only an old-timer driving a buggy, and him well back. On the sidewalk two hard-faced, gun-hung men looked up, studying him carefully as they heard the name.

"Sorry friend. You've got the wrong man," he replied.

The man grinned, a confidential sort of grin. The sort a man would give to a gentleman like Bad Bill Longley, if the latter did not wish his identity to be known. "Sure, Bill. I mean, sure mister."

Waco rode on without looking back, so he did not see the two men converge on the oldster. "Is that Longley?" the taller of the pair asked.

"Him?" The old-timer pushed back his hat and scratched his head. "Naw, it ain't Longley,"—but his tones confirmed that he thought it was.

Waco allowed his paint to make an easy pace along the street. He glanced at his reflection in a shop window. Six-foot odd of wide-shouldered, muscular and handsome young Texas cowhand looked back at him.

Texas—from the low-crowned wide-brimmed black JB Stetson hat, to the Kelly spurs on his boots. His multi-coloured bandana was long and tight-rolled, the ends hanging waist-long over his tan shirt. His levis were brown and new, hanging outside his high-heeled, fancy-stitched boots. Around his waist was a curved bus-cadero gunbelt, with matching staghorn butted Colt Artillery Peacemakers in the low-hanging holsters.

He turned the paint's head towards the livery barn and rode through the door, swinging down. A tall young man wearing a collarless shirt and tight-legged brown trousers came over, smiling a welcome.

"Howdy!" Waco greeted as he tied the thongs of his holsters, setting right the flaring butts with that un-conscious care which marked the practising gun-toter. "I'll take a stall for him—and don't let anyone touch him."

"You're telling me," the man looked at that seven-teen-hand paint with an eye for such things.

"That hotel across the street fit for a man to live in?"

"I couldn't say. I own it."

Waco grinned back, seeing the other was taking no offence at his caution in choosing a hotel. He led the horse into a stall and stripped off the heavy saddle. Then, after watering and feeding the big animal, he left it. He crossed the street and saw the two gunmen stand-ing watching him. He ignored them as he went on to the hotel porch, then through the open door.

The hotel lounge was cool and shady after the early spring sun outside. Waco crossed to the desk and the sleepy-looking clerk looked up. He yawned and opened the register.

"Only one room, friend."

"Reckon I don't need more than one," Waco replied.

Taking the pen, Waco glanced at the door; the two men were there watching him and some perverse imp prompted him to write "W. Lon." then cross it out again and write "W. Smith." Then he tossed a ten-

dollar piece on the desk and picked up his saddle again.
The clerk came round from behind the desk and led him
upstairs on the first floor. Waco turned and looked
back. The two men were still standing watching him.
They crossed the hall to examine the register.

Inside the small room, Waco laid his saddle carefully
on its side and tossed his bed-roll on to the bed. He sat
down on the bed and checked his guns, opening his war-
bag to take out cleaning gear. That was a fool mistake,
signing the hotel register as if he was Longley travelling
incognito. Bad Bill Longley was not the sort of man a
peace-seeking young fellow would want any part of; so
even looking like him could wind up in trouble. Longley
was a noted Texas gunfighter, fast as chain-lightning
and capable of downing his man with skill and pre-
cision.

Waco's month trip separate from his friends was so
far pleasant. He visited Clay Allison up at the Washita
country and, after a week with his old boss, moved on.
Now, with a week in hand, he was only fifty miles from
Tensonville and the end of his travels alone. He missed
the other members of Old Devil Hardin's floating outfit; but most particularly he knew he missed Dusty Fog.
The youngster knew all too well the path he'd been
following before he met the Rio Hondo gun-wizard. It
was one which could have led to his being a hunted
outlaw, or a hired killer. Now he was respectable and
respected. To Dusty Fog, he gave loyalty, hero-worship
and devotion which would have belonged to his father,
had not Waco Indians left him an orphan almost from
birth.

The youngster lay back on his bed, eyes half-closed,
thinking of the good times they'd had together, the
floating outfit. He looked round the room, it was small,
clean and neat. The bed was fairly comfortable, and the
sheets were clean. The only other furnishings were a
small table and a washstand.

Waco rolled from off his bed and looked from the

window. It was fast becoming dark by that time, so he picked up his hat and left, locking the door behind him. At the top of the stairs, he halted and looked down.

The two gunmen were standing just inside the doorway of the hotel, the taller one talking to a stocky, soberly dressed young man with a pugnacious, handsome face. The young man's back was to Waco; and the Texan could see a low-tied, ivory-butted Colt in a gunfighter's rig.

"Three more days, Marshall. That all!" The taller, a buck-toothed, unshaven man wearing dirty range clothes, was speaking as Waco came nearer. "And ole Pete Walls will be out and looking for you."

The second man—short, stocky and heavily-built, with a thick beard hiding his features, and a gun in a half-breed holster—went on: "You and ole Pete were about even afore he went to jail. Hear you're not so fast any more."

"Whyn't you try me and find out?" the stocky young man inquired softly, his hand lifting.

"Us?" the taller man grinned. "We ain't trying nobody, friend. Pete passed the word he wanted you."

Waco walked down the stairs. He saw the shorter gunman nudge his friend and they fell back. He walked on by them, not knowing nor caring the meaning of this by-play.

The street of the town was more crowded now, men coming in riding in wildly shouting groups; men with the aspect of cowhands, with pay in their pockets and the desire to spend it in their hearts. Waco watched the groups as they went by laughing and talking amongst themselves, and he felt lonely. If the other members of the floating outfit were here, they would be in the thick of the fun—as they often were at either Polveroso City or Diggers Wells, in the Rio Hondo. True, Waco would have been accepted by any of these outfits, and might even find someone he knew if he looked hard enough; but that night he did not want to make fresh friends.

One saloon sign caught his eye among the others. To a son of the Lone Star State, it came like shade and water in the desert.

"Texas House. That's for me," he said, and crossed the street. Behind him, the town marshal came from the hotel and watched him.

The saloon was no different from many another in the range country, Waco thought as he pushed through the batwing doors. The big bar-room presented the same garish, glaring mass of colour—for cowhands were not the quietest dressers in the world. The tables were crowded and, from the various games, could be heard shouts of encouragement, gambling terms and curses from the unlucky players. The bar was crowded with men, only a small gap having been left at one end. It was to this that Waco went. After some time he attracted the attention of one of the pair of leathery oldsters who now served behind it, after a long life of chasing Texas longhorns.

"Beer, cold and long, colonel," Waco greeted as one of the pair came along. "And a poker game."

"Get you the beer, but I ain't toting a poker table here for you," the bar-dog replied. "What game you got in mind?"

Waco felt the money in his pockets hanging heavily, and wanted to try his luck. His room was paid for, and he was free for a week from all cares; besides, he'd taken the precaution of leaving ten dollars in the room—so, even if he was fool enough to lose all in his pockets, he still would not be too close to the blanket.

"Not big, just friendly."

The bar-dog appraised him for a moment with shrewd eyes, then jerked his thumb to a small table in the side of the room. Four men were already playing at it, but there was an empty chair there.

"That do you?"

Waco took his beer and crossed the room, observing his future opponents as he came towards them. One he'd seen before—the well-dressed old-timer who'd mistaken him for Bad Bill Longley. Now he wore an older suit and his sun-bronzed face was wet with perspiration as he studied his cards. The man who sat next to him was a thin, small townsman, wearing a black vest and a white shirt with elbow protectors. The other two players could be nothing but travelling salesmen. Their loud check suits and derby hats told that. One was big, florid-faced and laughing loudly; the other silent, morose and moody.

"Room for players?"

Four pairs of eyes looked up, taking in every detail of the young man. It was the big drummer who replied for the others: "Chair's there—pull and set. I'm Brandy O'Hearne, 'cause I sell it. This here's Fred Jessop from the Telegraph office." The thin man in the white shirt nodded. "Amos Claypole from the store." The oldster winked at Waco. "And Ernie Copley."

"Folks call me Waco," the young man sat down in between Jessop and Copley, watching the other men.

The table was very small, in fact it would never have been used for a poker game unless the others were all full. The players were fairly close together and any one of them could reach clear across to the man facing him.

O'Hearne took the cards. Waco, alert as always, noted the way he held the deck, three fingers firmly gripping the long edge and the index finger curled round the shorter edge towards the centre of the table. That was a way of holding cards which few honest men practised—very handy for extracting cards from the bottom, or just under the top card, of the deck.

The cards flipped out fast, falling in front of the players while O'Hearne boomed out a continuation of his disreputable adventures. "Then her husband comes into the room," he explained as the cards flipped from his hands. "And he says, 'Now what steps are you taking?' and I says: 'Long ones.' "

"You dealt me six cards."

Waco's soft-spoken words cut across the table, bringing an end to the loud voice. Four pairs of eyes concentrated on him as he spread the cards. At first there only appeared to be five cards; but he took the third and squeezed it between thumb and forefinger. A second card slid from under it.

"Sorry, stranger," O'Hearne grunted.

"Cards must be getting sticky," Claypole remarked. "We'd best have us a new deck."

A passing waiter stopped and Jessop asked him for a new deck, then turned Waco's hand over. The cards were a middle high straight. "Hard luck, Waco. You would have been set with them."

Waco did not reply; he knew that he was supposed to bet on that hand, not knowing there were six cards in it. Then, on the call O'Hearne would expose the hand as having a card too many and the pot would be forfeit. The Texan knew that O'Hearne was playing crooked and guessed that Copley was his partner. Proof of this came when the man lay his hand open on the table in a casual manner—which told any one schooled in the signs of crooked gambling that there was one asking if there was another present.

Waco saw and understood the sign, but his face gave no sign of it. He'd started his training while helping Dusty Fog bring law to Mulrooney, Kansas. His teacher was an honest gambler who naturally needed to know such things to protect himself. The youngster showed his usual aptitude for learning and, on returning to the OD Connected, received further instruction from one of Ole Devil's friends—who made his living by gambling all over the West.

He watched everything, knowing that the two crooks were still not sure if he'd spotted them. Copley was the smoother manipulator of the cards and O'Hearne's loud talk and bluster served to act as a cover for him. Copley's casual picking up of the discards gave Waco a warning. The man moved fast and collected the cards, but he slid four kings together. Breaking the deck he gave them a riffle together, the cards flipping through his fingers fast, then slowing as he came to the place where the kings were grouped. Twice more he riffled and, while O'Hearne boomed out one of the stories of his illicit love affairs, Copley crimped the pack, making an almost imperceptible bend where he wanted the deck split in the cut. He lay the cards in front of O'Hearne.

Waco's hand slapped down hard, full on top of the deck at the end of the story, and before the drummer could cut. "Waal, I swan!" the young Texan whooped. "If that just don't beat all, Brandy. You're the lovingest man I ever saw."

O'Hearne's face lost its smile as he cut the deck. The vital crimp which was to help him had been flattened by the slap. The smile was even less in evidence when Waco took the hand with three of the kings.

The game went on. Jessop and Claypole could tell the different atmosphere now; there was a brittle tension and, although O'Hearne still made his jokes, his booming laughter was no longer rich and full. Copley was getting more and more angry all the time, as the pile of chips in front of the three would-be suckers grew, while his own and O'Hearne's shrank accordingly.

Hand followed hand. Waco played carefully, never betting—no matter how good his cards—when Copley dealt. He knew the two men were suspicious of him —but they were still unable to decide if he was on to them, or just plain lucky. He watched them signal to each other, reading the code and knowing when one wanted the other to hike up the betting, or signalled for a special card. In some way, Claypole and Jessop caught on to what he was doing and followed his lead like hound-dogs running a hot scent; so, all in all, the two card-sharps caught a very lean time of it.

Then Waco saw what he was waiting for, the riffle stock again laid the four kings in position and, this time Copley gave Waco no chance of knocking his crimp out of the deck. The young Texan picked up his cards, fanning them out; and he grinned inside as he saw that he held an ace among the other cards. In the last few hands, there had been a lack of aces showing—which was not surprising, for Waco held three of them tucked in the bend of his knee, extracted for just such a moment.

The betting round went on, Copley and O'Hearne pushing it up as high as they could. The deck lay in the centre of the table and Waco hitched his chair nearer, at the same time extracting the three aces. Then he knocked over a pile of chips and reached to pick them up, shoving the pack aside. The three aces now lay on top of the pack—all ready, eager and in place to be drawn by him.

"Cards?" Copley growled.

"Take three," Waco replied, tossing all but the ace and one other card on to the table.

Copley dealt, the three cards dropped in front of Waco and he scooped them up, fanning them carefully. Four fat, lovely aces now met his gaze, a far, far better hand than the four kings O'Hearne drew one card to.

The betting rose. At last, only O'Hearne and Waco were left, and the big drummer laughed. "I'll make it easy on you. See them."

He beamed round and tossed the four kings down singly in front of him. The grin faded as Waco replied: "This bullet kills him," and tossed an ace on to the first king. "And him and him and poor lil ole him."

Copley stared at the cards, knowing that he would have noticed the three aces being together in his casual check through of the deck when he was waiting to deal. Then he snarled: "What's the game?"

"Poker, they tell me," Waco replied.

"Don't get flip with me," Copley hissed. "There's something funny about the way you play."

Copley and O'Hearne pushed back their chairs. The

big man held a pile of chips in his left hand. Claypole
looked up at them both, then softly said: "This-here's
Bad Bill Longley."

The name stiffened both men. Then Copley looked at
the pile of chips, almost all their stakes, in the centre of
the table. He nodded. O'Hearne sent the stack of chips
across the table and, at the same moment, Copley's
hand went under his coat. The two moves were well-
planned and should have warranted more success than
they gained. Instead of glancing down at the chips,
Waco ignored them, his matched guns coming out an instant before Copley's Remington double derringer slid
clear. The left-hand gun threw a bullet into Copley's
shoulder, knocking him backwards from his feet.
O'Hearne snarled a curse and started his draw. The left-
hand gun came round and up, its barrel smashing full
into the fat throat.

The crowd were up on their feet and several men
made motions towards their guns; but Waco came
round in a smooth turn, his Colts making an arc of the
room. "Now all hold it!" he ordered.

A well-dressed man stepped forward, hands held
shoulder high and a placating look on his face. "Like to
say that, as the owner of this place, I never saw these
two before."

The staghorn-handled guns went back into leather
again, dropping into their niches with the casual flip
which told that here was a master hand with a gun.
Waco then nodded and informed the crowd that they
might resume their interrupted games. Then he saw the
young marshal crossing the room.

"What happened, Fred?" the Marshal asked. He
looked at Copley, who was on his knees, holding his
bloody shoulder, and at O'Hearne, who was desperately
trying to work his throat and get air flowing properly
again.

"These two are a pair of sharps, Duke. I knew it soon

as I started playing. Meant to cut out, but Longley here called them," Jessop replied. "For a cowhand, he handles a mean deck of cards."

"Cowhand!" Copley snarled out through his pain-wracked lips. "He's a professional tinhorn."

Duke Tavener ignored the remark. He snapped: "You pair be out of town on the stage tomorrow. Until then, keep in your room. If I see you out I'll throw you in jail."

The two drummers left, O'Hearne supporting his friend, heading for the doctor. Tavener watched them go, then turned and looked Waco upon and down. "Are you Bill Longley?"

"He surely is," Claypole put in, before Waco could speak. "Knowed him last time he was in this area."

"There's no warrant out for him in New Mexico."

"Nor likely to be," Waco replied, watching the young lawman.

"You're right. I want you out of this town before dawn."

"I paid a week at the hotel." Waco saw something in the lawman's eyes. It wasn't fear or anything he could tie down.

Tavener moved back, hand lifting slightly, the look still in his eyes. "What I said still goes."

There was once a time in Waco's young life when he would have welcomed this chance to draw and shoot. Now he thought, and acted, differently.

"Hold hard, Marshal. You don't know for sure that I'm Longley."

"I don't care—just be out of town or I'll jail you."

The crowd in the saloon watched, moving back out of the possible line of fire. Every eye was on the small group in the centre of the room. They were all wondering if this man they thought to be the Mill Creek terror would draw; and if Duke Tavener could beat him to the shot.

Waco knew these thoughts. He also knew that, if he even wounded the young lawman, Tavener was done for as a marshal. So Waco made a decision which would have amazed any man who'd known him in the days when he rode for Clay Allison.

"I don't want any trouble with you, Marshal. I'll go along to the jail with you and talk it out."

Tavener stared at the tall young Texan for a long moment. Then he nodded in agreement. "Let's go."

Waco led the way from the saloon and, behind him, Claypole shouted: "There you are, boys. Who said Duke Tavener was scared? Even Bad Bill Longley wouldn't face up to him."

Out on the street, Waco jerked a thumb towards two men coming from a saloon further along. He unbuckled the heavy gun-belt and swung it back to Tavener. "Here, make like you're taking me to jail."

Tavener took the belt, hardly knowing what to make of this action. He followed the Texan, walking in the position a lawman would when escorting a prisoner. The two gunmen glanced at Tavener and Waco as they passed, then stared again. The short man dropped his smoke and the other's eyes bugged out. They stared after the pair, until they entered the jail.

"You're not Bill Longley," Tavener stated as he handed Waco back the gun-belt.

"Nope."

"I'm not doubting you any. I don't know what Claypole was doing. He knew Bad Bill five years back and described him just as you look."

" 'Cepting Bad Bill'd be five years older," Waco pointed out. "I know him—he's kin to the Ysabel Kid."

The jail door was thrown open and three prosperous-looking men came in, led by a big, hearty-looking man with a sun-reddened face, but soft white hands. He was the spokesman for the others:

"So it's true you brought Longley in."

"Sure, Banker Darcy. Didn't you think I could?" Tavener replied.

"Why Duke?" Darcy looked at Waco, who sat at the desk. "He won't forget this, and you've got enough on your hands with Pete Walls coming back here."

"The thing is, Duke," Darcy put in. "We think that it would be best for the town if you took a vacation until Walls has gone."

"Run, you mean. Like my deputy ran?"

"He showed good sense," another man snapped. "Walls will start hoorawing the town again, when he comes back. But he might go easier, if you aren't here."

Tavener scowled, his eyes on the other three. "With or without a badge. I'm staying on."

"It'll be with a badge, as long as I have any say," Darcy barked.

"No one suggested we took Duke's badge," the second man objected—in a tone which showed that it had been suggested. "But folks don't like the idea of Walls coming here and hunting Duke."

"Get me a deputy, and I might be able to stop him," Tavener said softly. "Even if he does have Matt Chandler riding with him."

The three men looked at each other. Darcy spoke again for them: "I've tried, Duke; he tried. No one will take on after what happened to your deputy. The town is scared of Walls."

The three men turned and walked out. As they did so, a plump, pretty young woman pushed by them and into the jail office. Waco looked her over; her hair was blonde, short and curly, her face that innocent, warm and babyish kind a plump woman often had. It was a face made for smiling, not for the raw, aching fear it showed right then.

"It was true then, Duke," she said, "Why do you do it?"

"Do what, honey?"

"Face down men like this"—she waved a hand to the impassive young Texan. "This whole town isn't worth it."

Tavener took the young woman's hands and Waco saw the wedding ring on the left. "This isn't Longley."

"I know he isn't," she replied. "But he's one of the good guns. Don't tell me, Duke. I've seen them. He's one." She turned to Waco. "Did you know that my husband can't use his thumb well enough to cock a Colt?"

"Lindy!" Tavener snapped. "You shouldn't have said that——"

"Why not?" she replied, her blue eyes near to tears. "It's the truth. You got frost-bitten in the blue norther and you can't work your thumb."

Waco strapped his guns on, rising to his feet. "I'll be going. Hope I helped you a mite."

The woman looked up at Waco, then at her husband.

Tavener nodded. "Yes. He came because he wanted to, not because I scared him. Gave me his guns when he saw Krag and Hellem in the street. I don't know why."

"Dusty Fog always told me to help the law when I could. Thought it might give you a boost, if folks thought you'd brought Longley in," Waco explained.

"Will you be Duke's deputy?"

"Listen, Lindy!" Tavener barked. "You can't ask a man to fight my battles for me. I——"

"Only for three days, unless this young man wants to stay on. The folks in town are scared of Pete Walls. They may get their guts back, if they think Bill Longley is backing you."

"We can't ask a man to fight for us," Tavener objected. "I've got my pride."

"Happen they'll put it on your tombstone," Waco put in. "I don't know what's coming off in this town, but I surely need a riding chore."

"Krag and Hellem beat up my last man," Tavener

warned. Then he remembered the two drummers at the saloon. "I reckon you can take care of yourself. You mentioned Dusty Fog?"

"I ride for Ole Devil's floating outfit," Waco answered and, despite her fear and anxiety, Lindy Tavener smiled at the obvious pride in his tones. "Name's Waco. You tell me all about it."

Duke Tavener took a seat and Waco pulled up on the other side of the desk. Meanwhile, Lindy went to the stove and set a coffee-pot on it.

"Pete Walls ran a spread out there in the range country. When some of his cows appeared with two calves, folks didn't say much. He used to hooraw the town and kept most folks treed. Town was booming wide open and he rode with a bunch of real tough men. Then, when all his cows had three or four calves each, and even the bulls had a couple, folks got riled. They elected me Marshal. I got a posse and we went after Walls. We caught him dead to rights. I snuck up and buffaloed him and we got the rest. Walls pulled eight years in the Territory Pen, and swore he'd get me when he came out."

"He'll be out and here in three days," Lindy spoke from the stove.

Waco was fitting the pattern together. He asked, "Who knows about your hand?"

"Only two people, Lindy and you. I've tamed this town down and never needed to use a gun since the frostbite," Tavener answered. "It was wild, but I managed to tame it. There are a few in town who think it is too tame. The don't make the kind of money they used to in the old days. Well, a fortnight back, Krag and Hellem, two of Wall's men who we couldn't pin anything on, started to come to town again. They behaved and just hung around, telling me how long it would be before Walls came back. I can't even prove they worked my deputy over. He wouldn't talk. They just stay on here."

"Didn't look like they were eager to match shots with you," Waco remarked.

"They aren't. Yet. Walls wants to handle me himself."

Waco was thinking again, his brain racing over what he knew. He turned every aspect over in his mind and asked a question: "How would you and Walls stack up in a shooting match?"

"We were about equal—that was why the town elected me Marshal."

"Where did Walls's guns go?"

"The County sold most of his effects. I kept his Colt in the safe here—don't know why."

"Hodgkiss wouldn't let it be sold for the price offered at the auction," the woman put in. "He's the town undertaker and was on the Town Council—until the better class of citizen turned him off. He is one who doesn't like the idea of a clean town. We had at least one killing a week here until the clean-up; his business isn't so good now."

Waco rose and paced the room. He stopped at the desk again. "I can't stay more than the three or four days, unless Walls doesn't come. I have to be in Tensonville before the end of the week. I'll go across to the hotel and get some sleep, unless you want me to take first round of the town."

Tavener handed over a deputy's badge and watched the young man pin it to his calfskin vest. After Waco left the room, the Taveners looked at each other. "He's held a badge before," Lindy remarked.

"Sure. Looks like I've got me a deputy who'll stick."

Waco was the first man in the hotel dining-room the following morning. A sleepy-eyed woman served him breakfast and, while he was eating it, the young man from the livery barn came in and joined him.

"Morning, Mr. Longley," he greeted. "See you're staying on here."

"Looks that way."

"Some of the boys are a mite rough on deputies—not that it would worry you. I saw you in the Texas House. My name's Jack Walls."

"Kin to Pete?"

"Nodding kin is all," Walls answered wryly. "We never took to each other. I was with Duke the night we arrested him. He'll be coming back real soon and looking for Duke. And me."

"Folks back Duke up?"

"Some will, now. Pete was a good man with a gun. So are some of his boys. Word has it he's hired Matt Chandler, too."

"Chandler?" Waco finished his breakfast and rolled a smoke. "I've heard about him, some."

"Some?" Walls stared across the table. "He's the fastest man alive, even faster than Dusty Fog."

"He's not. There is only one man who can shade Dusty, and none who can lick him with a brace."

The door of the room was thrown open and man came in fast. "Mr. Longley, a bunch of cowhands are fixing to wreck the undertaker's shop."

Waco rose and left. He saw the trouble-spot with no eyestrain; a fair crowd was gathered outside and he watched them scatter to allow him through. The shop was dimly-lit but there was enough light for Waco to see what was going on. A thin, miserable-looking man in sober black cowered back at the counter, while several young cowhands crowded forward at him.

"Hold it, gents!"

The cowhands turned slightly, all looking at the tall shape in the doorway. One of them held a gun. He started to turn.

"Pouch it!" Waco snapped.

"Who're you?" the cowhand asked.

"You deaf?" The twin staghorn-butted guns were out and lined in a flicker of movement. "I said put it away!"

The gun went back into leather, and the cowhand watched for the next development. He knew there was a new lawman in town; and, although Duke Tavener was fair, the hands wanted to know how this new man would be.

"One of you'd better tell it," Waco suggested.

"Ole Eph there got himself drunk last night and just passed away. So we got to figgering it would be a good joke to tote him across here and put him in one of Hodgkiss's coffins. It war—only, when he woke, he'd lost an eighty-dollar roll from his pocket."

Waco glanced at a tall, gangling man, who looked as if he was suffering the tortures of the damned. He lifted himself from where he was lounging on the counter and ambled forward, but Hodgkiss put his spoke in first.

"Arrest these men, deputy!"

"On what charge?"

"They broke into my shop," Hodgkiss snapped back.

"Why, you damned ole goat—the door wasn't locked. You allus leave it open, you're so scared of losing a chance to make money," the cowhand yelled back. "We just toted ole Eph in here last night. You came out just afore he did."

Waco turned his attention to Eph and asked to hear his side of it. "I woke up this morning, felling that I'd be better dead—and I surely ain't going to get drunk again. War comfortable and there was two lil men sat on my head, holding my eyes closed. Then, when I felt somebody in my pocket, I opened 'em—and found I was in a coffin."

The young cowhand who'd acted as spokesman gave a whoop of delight. "He sure did. Ole Eph howled like a stuck shoat and jumped clear out of that ole pinewood box. I tell you, Marshall, his feet never touched the floor until he was out in the sun again."

"About the money?" Waco went on doggedly.

"It's for the ranch supplies," Eph answered. "War in my pocket."

"That's right, Marshal," the other hand agreed. "I checked afore I left. But I figgered it would be safer with him than me."

Hodgkiss's thin face worked angrily. He scowled at the men and snarled: "You arrest them, all of them."

"Not so fast. This thing's settled a damned sight easier than that. I'll search the men who toted Eph in here. And you."

The cowhands agreed to this willingly enough, but Hodgkiss snorted and took a step back. "I won't be searched."

"Then I'll take you to jail, inciting a riot we'll call it."

"What?" Hodgkiss almost screeched. "You can't do that to me. I'll have your badge for this."

"Sure. But, until you do, I'm still the law here."

"Not in my shop."

"All right." Waco turned on his heel. "You boys just carry on."

"Wait!" Hodgkiss saw the eager looks on the faces of the cowhands. "I found this money on the floor of the shop and thought the man who ran out as I came in dropped it." He pulled out a roll of money and handed it to Eph. "He must have been robbing you."

"Why you scraggy ole vulture!" Eph growled angrily, starting forward. Waco stopped him.

"You've got your money, friend, so go buy your supplies. I'll arrest Mr. Hodgkiss if you like, but there isn't a thing we could make stick. He was fair enough to stop that feller robbing you, and he's forgotten all about you damaging his merchandise. Leave it lie, friend."

The cowhands agreed with Waco; they could see that here was a fair lawman and one who was worth backing. Hodgkiss grumbled a little and watched Waco leave the shop with eyes that were full of hatred. He found little support for his complaints among the other people to whom he talked. They knew him as a sanctimonious skinflint who was quite capable of rolling a drunk if he was given the chance. They also were not going against a man like Bad Bill Longley.

Duke Tavener was in the jail when Waco finished the rounds and entered. The Marshal looked far happier than before; the worried, desperate look was almost gone from his eyes.

"You riled Mr. Hodgkiss. He's some annoyed."

Waco removed his hat and looked piously at the roof. "I mourns for Mr. Hodgkiss. And does the aforesaid Mr. Hodgkiss want me fired?"

"He does that. Swore he'd go to the Town Council and use his influence. What do I call you?"

"Bill, or Longley—if anyone's around. Waco's what I answer to most times."

"You mentioned Dusty Fog, and Ole Devil Hardin's floating outfit."

Waco told the amused Tavener about the bet; and insisted that he'd only taken the job here because he'd lost the bet by getting into the fight. Then the Marshal pointed out that he'd won a fair sum at the Texas House and left it on the table. Claypole himself brought the money in that morning.

"For a man who's short of money, you're sure careless with what you've got," Tavener finished up. "I told Mr. Hodgkiss I'd talk real sharp to you. Consider it done."

"Sure. Now we've got to see about getting you ready to face Pete Walls. I want to see how fast you are."

They both unloaded their guns, then dropped them back into leather. Standing facing each other, they dropped their hands. Waco's guns came clear, hammers earing back ready. Duke Tavener was fast; yet his draw did not have that extra flicker of speed which threw him into the class of the top guns. His draw alone was fast, his thumb was stiff and awkward, not earing back the hammer as was necessary with a Colt single-action revolver.

"Any place we can do some shooting?" Waco asked

after they reloaded their guns.

"Sure, there's a draw at the back of my house. We can go down there."

In the draw behind the house stood an old wooden shack, its walls pock-marked with bullet-holes. With a piece of chalk. Waco drew a rough outline shaped like a man. On the left side, he drew a heart shape, then stepped back.

"Ever try fanning a gun, Duke?" he asked.

"Sure, just for laughs. There's no accuracy in fanning."

"Wouldn't say that," Waco disagreed. "You can't do any fancy shooting with it. But at killing range you can hit."

He stepped back about twenty feet from the target. Then his right hand went down, the Colt coming clear and locking tight up against his side while his left hand fanned the hammer back. Five shots sounded as fast as the roll of a drum. When the smoke rolled away, they went to look at the target. Four of the shots were grouped in the heart, the other was two inches above it.

"Man, that's what I call shooting," Tavener stated as he laid a hand over the holes, covering them. "It must have taken you plenty of time to learn how to do it."

"Some. But we've only got us three days right now. Take your gun out slow and ram your elbow tight into your side. Get that habit first."

Duke Tavener tried, taking the gun out slow and, instead of thrusting it out, held it squarely in the center of his body. He rammed his elbow into his side hard. Then the heel of his left brought back the hammer and fired. The bullet struck in the target area.

After about an hour of practice, Waco and Tavener called it a day; or, at least, gave it a rest for a time. The Marshal shook his head, "I don't know if it'll work. But I've no other choice."

"Longley!" The voice brought Waco to a halt as he

returned from attending to his horse. He turned to find Krag and Hellem facing him. "What you doing wearing a badge?"

"I like wearing it. Makes hard men who don't like lawmen come after me."

Krag moved to the right and Hellem to the left, watching him. Krag, the taller, went on: "Hear tell you're a real maneater in Texas. This ain't Texas."

"It ain't," Waco agreed. "You pair think I'm no good here?"

Hellem sneered: "Funny how tough they get when they're behind a badge."

Waco's right hand lifted to remove the badge. At the same moment, Hellem went for his gun. Waco shot him through the shoulder with the gun which came into his left hand, slamming him backwards on to the sidewalk. Krag's hand stopped inches from his gun as the Colt lined on him.

The Colt whirled on Waco's trigger-finger and went back into leather as he faced Krag. "Go on, hard man, pull it!"

Krag licked his lips, looking at Hellem, who was down and groaning in pain. "You got me all wrong, Bill."

Waco moved in, his right hand slapping hard across the man's face, knocking him from his feet. "Mister, get out of this town. The next time I see you, there'll be shooting. Two of you gents take this *hombre* to the doctor. Get him patched up and tell him to clear town fast."

Duke Tavener arrived at a run; he watched Krag walking away and two men helping Tellem in the direction of the doctor's office. "What happened?" he asked.

"Justa couple of gents who decided they didn't like lawmen," Waco answered. "Which same they tried real hard to prove."

"Hellem was more than fair with a gun." Tavener's voice was low, talking more to himself than to his deputy.

"Tolerable, only tolerable. We use faster'n him for the young'uns to start on back home to Texas."

"Huh, you can always tell a Texan," Duke grunted disgustedly.

"Sure, but you can't tell us much."

They walked on together to the jail and entered the office.

"All right, Duke. I want to see you draw again," Waco said again.

Duke rose, unloading his guns and slipping empty cartridge cases into the chambers. This was to protect the firing-pin on the hammer—for repeated dropping on a empty cylinder could smash the pin and damage the hammer. His hand went down, the gun coming out; and, through sheer instinct, he tried to thumb the hammer back.

"That's no good," Waco snapped. "Keep thinking about fanning the hammer. Keep it on your mind all the time. Draw, then slap back the hammer hard. You've got but two more days to learn."

"If I don't?"

"Then Pete Walls will do what you wanted me to do last night."

Tavener looked at the Texan's expressionless face. For a moment he was silent, then asked: "How did you know what I wanted to happen?"

"It figgers. You've been living on raw nerves for weeks. Last night you saw a chance to end it, one way or another. So you aimed to make Bad Bill Longley go against you and end the waiting for good."

Tavener paced the room. He halted and looked down at Waco. "You're a smart young feller."

The door of the jail opened and Darcy came in. He beamed at Tavener and Waco and dabbed perspiration from his face. "Just came by to ask if you want any more deputies."

"*Could* I get more?" Tavener asked, remembering the night before.

"Near on every man in town'll stand by you."

"Me—or Bad Bill Longley?"

"Both. Oh, I know we've been kind of slow offering to help, but you know how it is."

"Sure." There was a touch of bitterness in Duke's tones. "I know how it is. I'll let you know about the deputies."

Waco watched the banker leave before he spoke: "Folks are funny, I reckon. They know that you and Walls were about equal with a gun. It is the rest of his bunch that spooks them."

He walked across the room, looking down at the floor. The jail had not been swept in the past couple of days, so there was a layer of dust over it, marked with footprints. He halted in front of the safe, looking down at the ground. The Ysabel Kid was a tracker with few equals, and he'd taught Waco much. Enough to know those footprints in front of the safe door did not belong there, nor were they Tavener's. He, himself, had not been near the safe before. The young Texan looked at the lock and tested the handle. Then he returned to the table.

"Who had a key to the safe?"

"Myself. There's a spare at home and the town council usually have one. Why?"

"Curious. We use the same system down in the Rio Hondo," Waco replied. "I reckon I'll stay on at the jail all night, bunk down in a cell."

"Why?" Tavener tried to read something in that bronzed handsome young face.

"Just too tired to walk up the hotel stairs. Say, can I put my money in the safe? I'm likely to get into another poker game and lose it all if I don't."

Duke tossed Waco a key and the young man went to open the small safe. He looked in. The top shelf was empty, but the second held two guns—one was an old, beat-up Remington; the other a well-cared for, clean and oiled Colt. Waco felt relieved. He shut the door again, but did not leave his money inside.

"Let's get us back to practising that fanning again," he said.

There was a marked difference in the attitude of the people in town when Tavener made his rounds that night. The faces which had been tense and scared were smiling and friendly again. Several times he received offers of help when Walls came back, but refused them all. He saw his deputy once, coming from the store and carrying a small package; but Waco did not offer to explain what was in it, so he didn't press it any.

It was shortly before midnight when they met again at the jail. Tavener came in and found Waco sitting at the desk. "Still thinking of sleeping down here?" he asked.

"Sure, no sense in going back to the hotel."

Tavener shrugged; he didn't know what was worrying Waco and did not want to pry into things which were none of his concern. For a moment, he wondered if the young Texan was getting scared and wanting to get out of his arrangement. If that was to happen, the town would fold in and run. Yet there was no sign of fear in any part of Waco's attitude—and in the last few weeks Tavener had become a student of fear in others.

After the Marshal left, Waco rose and crossed the room. He opened his package and shook flour over the floor in front of the safe, leaving it lying thick and smooth. Then he left the jail and made a quick round of the town. One thing he'd found out earlier on was that Hodgkiss was a frugal man who went to bed early and lived at the back of his shop. It was surprising that this night there was a crack of light showing from his window.

The cell bed was hard and not conducive to deep slumber, but this was what Waco wanted. He was a light sleeper, unless in the safe confines of his own bed at the OD Connected. He was asleep as soon as his head hit the pillow. Some time went by and Waco slept in the darkened jail. At around four, the door opened slowly, and a smallish, dark shape came from the street, crossing the room towards the safe. The visitor, who-ever he was, was good; he made scarcely a sound as he crossed the floor.

Waco rolled from his bed; his stockinged feet made no sound either as they hit the floor. He hefted his right hand gun and, as the safe door creaked open, snapped: "Hold it there!"

The man at the safe was fast, real fast. He came round and flame blossomed from the barrel of a gun. The bullet struck a cell bar and flying chips of metal stung Waco's cheek, making him flinch. He hit the ground fast, rolling under the bunk and holding his fire, for the other man was moving fast.

Waco stayed where he was, breathing gently and try-ing to see the other man. He watched the door opening and silently promised to get anyone coming through it. Then there was a rush of silent feet and a smashing of glass as the other man went through the window, diving low and shattering the glass in all directions.

Waco dived from under the bed; he got off two fast took shots but knew neither were hits. Outside, he heard the sound of running feet fading away, and darted across the room to crash his leg into the desk. The pain brought him to a halt, wild and lurid oaths pouring from his lips. Then he stopped and listened; the man was still on foot. In this quiet, a horse would make a noise that could be heard a fair distance away.

"Waco!" It was Duke Tavener's voice shouting from the darkness. The Marshal had been worried by Waco's staying on at the jail and, instead of going to bed, had dozed in his chair, fully-dressed. The shots had attracted his attention and brought him from the house at a dead run; but he'd more sense than to barge in on his deputy in the dark without shouting a warning.

"Come ahead!" Waco called back as he struck a match and lit the lamp on the desk.

Entering the office, Tavener looked around, then down at the flour in front of the safe. The layer of flour was marked by footprints and a line led towards the door, made by flour-stained feet. The safe door was open. Tavener went to it and looked in, then turned. His eyes took in Waco's unsmiling face.

"Took your money, and both guns."

"Only the old gun. I kept my money with me," Waco replied.

"What's it all about, Waco?"

"I figgered that someone tried to open the safe last night, only they didn't have a key. Then I figgered they might try again, so I baited a trap."

"Where would they get the key from?"

"I don't know for sure, so I'm not saying. But I reckon it could have been from any member of the Council, past and present. They all have keys."

"They turn the key in when they retire," Tavener remarked. "That means it's one of the present council."

"Why, a man can get a spare key cut easy enough. Man like I suspect would do it just on the chance that he might need it some time," Waco answered and pulled the door round. A key was still in the lock. He removed this, holding it out. "This one of the regular keys? I didn't figger he'd time to take it out."

Tavener took the key out of the lock and glanced at it, then pulled his own out and compared them. "Nope. These are the maker's keys. The other is homemade —no maker's mark or anything."

Waco accepted the key and turned it over in his hands. "Take a good man to turn one of these out. Who could do it?"

"Hodgkiss makes keys," Tavener replied. "He was a friend of Pete Walls—or, at least, as friendly as Hodgkiss ever gets with anyone. You suspect him?"

"I'm suspecting, not saying," Waco replied. "Waal, I reckon I'll sleep the night out."

Tavener watched the young Texan return to the cell and get on the bed. Then he grinned and left. Waco was acting mysterious; but somehow, he didn't mind. He turned and, after blowing out the lamp, left the room to walk along the street. His hand dropped and the gun came out, but his instinct still made him try to work the hammer with his stiff thumb. He licked his lips, returned the gun to leather again and walked on. His sole chance when Pete Walls came was to be able to remember what Waco was trying to teach him. He had to get rid of the habit of a lifetime in a very short period, and learn an entirely different style of shooting.

The morning was quiet, clear and fine. Duke Tavener sat in the jail office with his deputy, talking softly. The marshal was no nearer finding out what Waco had been up to the previous night, and he wasn't even trying to find out.

"Tavener!" a voice shouted. "Come on out here."

Tavener and Waco went to the door of the jail. A middle-sized man with a hard-looking, scarred face sat a shaggy-looking cowhorse outside the jail. A crowd was gathering around, all watching the man.

"Howdy, Brennan. Haven't seen you around before," Tavener replied. "What're you wanting here?"

"Got a message from Pete Walls," the man replied. "He'll be coming in at noon, him and the boys. He's going to kill you, and burn this town to the ground."

"Him, or Matt Chandler, doing the killing?" Waco asked softly.

"Who're you?" Brennan growled.

"They call me Longley," Waco answered, looking down at the man's boots. "You been in town long?"

"Just come in."

"Then just get out again."

"Yeah?" Brennan grinned mockingly, his hand lifting.

Waco moved faster. His hands closed on the boot and heaved. With a yell, Brennan went over his saddle and crashed to the ground. Waco was after him, ducking under the head of the horse and kicking the gun from Brennan's hand. Duke Tavener pushed by Waco and dragged the man to his feet again. Brennan tried to get out his second gun, but a fist drove into his stomach doubling him over. Tavener let loose and stepped back a pace, then brought up a right which lifted the other man erect and slammed him into the hitching-rail. Brennan clung there, blood trickling from his mouth.

"Listen to me," Travener snapped. "You go back and tell Walls to stay out of town. If he comes, there'll be shooting."

"Yeah?" Brennan gasped out. "I'll do that. And you be here, Longley. Just be here, that's all I ask."

"I will. But this is between your boss and Duke. If you, Chandler, or any other man cuts in, so do I."

Brennan picked up his guns and shoved them back into leather again. Then, mounting his horse, he rode away from the front of the jail and headed out of town. Waco watched him go and a surge of people came round, the men eager to help out if there was need.

"How many of us do you need?" the hotel owner asked.

"None. This is between Pete and me. If there are a whole lot of you here, it will look as if he's got you scared."

"He'll have all four of his men, and Chandler," Darcy, the banker, put in.

"Three—Bill here put lead into Hellem," Tavener corrected. "You folks go home. I've got work to do here."

The crowd scattered and Tavener's wife went into the

jail. She looked round at the place and clucked her tongue. "What a mess! Who spilled all the flour on the floor?"

"Me, I reckon. That gent out there, he cleaned some of it up."

"He the one?"

"Sure, Duke. There was traces on his boot—under the instep, where he hadn't cleaned them. I don't reckon he's rid far. I'll just go check."

Waco left Tavener and his wife alone. Lindy was sweeping up the floor and the Texan wanted to take a walk. He went round the back of the houses, until he was behind the undertaker's place. It was surrounded by a board fence, but Waco found a crack wide enough to see through. The yard was littered with old pieces of wood, the hearse stood in a lean-to; and, opposite, was the undertaker's team. Each stall was full. Then Waco saw the horse droppings in the hearse lean-to. He gripped the top of the fence and pulled himself up, then swung over. Crossing the yard, he vent over to examine the droppings. His guess was right; they were new and certainly not left before the previous night. A horse had been tied there all night and, from the hair which was rubbed off on to the side of the hearse, the horse was a shaggy-coated bay such as Brennan was riding.

"I don't like it," a voice said from the other side of the fence as a gate in it opened further along.

Waco moved fast, diving under the hearse and rolling into the shadows at the back of the lean-to. He saw Hodgkiss and a lean, tough-looking cowhand enter the yard.

"You ain't being asked to like it," the cowhand replied. "Pete put some big money your way when he was in town, and he wants a favour doing."

"All right but this'd better go right," Hodgkiss answered. By then they were at the door of the business and, as they went in, Waco lost the rest of the talk.

He stayed for a time, then carefully moved round the hearse. Keeping close to the side of the lean-to, he climbed the fence.

Lindy and Duke Tavener looked up as their new-found friend entered. The young woman looked at his dirty clothes and asked: "What have you been doing to get like that?"

"Hiding!" Waco answered. "Half-past-ten, Duke. Get Lindy out of here to the house. I saw Banker Darcy. Him and Walls from the hotel are going to stay with her. Figgered it would be best, until this was over."

Tavener and his wife looked at each other, then both laughed. Lindy stopped first. "Waco, Duke and I have decided that this isn't your fight, and that you ought to keep out of it. Now you come here and tell me you've arranged for a guard for me. You beat all."

"You should head out—it'll be tough and dangerous," Tavener went on.

"I told you: I lost my bet and need to work for the money to pay it."

Taking out his wallet, Tavener dropped three ten-dollar bills on to the desk top. "There you are. That'll cover it."

Waco grinned, ignoring the money. "If I take that, I won't need to ride on. I can stay here and find another poker game."

Lindy snorted, half in anger, half in delight, at this calm young man. She shook her head and left the room. Two men crossed the street, one moving to either side of her. She looked at them; they were townsmen, old friends of her family and each toting a shotgun.

"Waco—I mean Longley?" she asked.

"Longley," one of the men agreed. "Tells us that we've got to take you home and stay here with banker Darcy."

Tavener looked at Waco for a long time after his wife left. "I'm scared," he finally said.

"So am I," Waco answered.

The Marshal studied the other's face, trying to read what was going on in his mind. "You don't look scared. Is it Chandler who's worrying you?"

"Nope. I'm scared they might not come and keep me on here. I want to get back with Dusty, Mark, the Kid and Red again. Talked to Darcy. He told me some about how this town was before you tamed it down. He knows that, if Walls isn't stopped, it will go the same way again. He's managed to get a whole lot of other folks behind him, and they'll back you."

"They're backing Bad Bill Longley."

Sure. And, when they see that you can handle Walls, they'll back you. I'll not even be a memory in a few months."

"Lindy and I will never forget you if, I get by today."

Waco grinned, he took a deck of cards from his pocket, opened the packet and tipped them out. "You'll get by." He riffled the cards. "Say, if you ever see a man holding the cards this way, watch him."

In a few moments, Waco, with his show of crooked gambling moves, took Duke Tavener's mind clean off the future. The clock on the wall ticked away as the two men sat facing each other across the desk, watching the cards, while the time rolled by for them to go out and either kill or die.

"They're coming!" A man stepped in through the door of the jail. "Saw them on the south trail."

"Thanks. Go pull in the others," Waco replied.

"Others?" Duke Tavener asked. "What others?"

"Longley got men on each trail, watching for them," the man explained.

Duke Tavener watched Waco checking his guns and shook his head. For one so young, the Texan was packed full of good common sense and didn't appear to have missed a trick.

Four men were swinging down from their horses along the deserted street; Krag, Brennan and two tall riders. One wore range clothes, but his face bore a pallor not in keeping with the tan of the others. The other also wore range clothes, but they were of an expensive cut and only the low-tied Colt gun at his side was not in line with his fancy dress. It was a fighting man's weapon, plain and worked on to give that extra speed so necessary.

They fanned out across the street, Krag at one side, Brennan at the other, Pete Walls and Matt Chandler in the middle. Along the street, Waco and Tavener left the jail, to move into the centre of the trail and wait for them.

"You said three, without Chandler," Waco said, speaking from the corner of his mouth and never taking his eyes from the men.

"Stanton's not with them," Tavener replied, keeping his mind focused on one thing: *Drop the hand, lift out the gun, then fan the hammer*.

The hair on the back of Waco's neck rose bristle-stiff. There, along the street behind them, was the undertaker's shop. In that shop was a man who shouldn't be there.

It was too late to do anything; the four men were in close now—halting and waiting for the next move. Then the pallid man spoke:

"Howdy, Duke. See you stayed on."

"Walls!" Before Duke could reply, a voice spoke from the side of the street.

Walls looked in the direction; several of the townsmen stood there holding either rifles or shotguns. "Well?" he asked.

"Figger it's between you and Duke. The rest of your men stay out."

"Yeah?" Matt Chandler spoke softly.

"Chandler!" Waco snapped. "Did you get my word?"

The hired killer looked Waco over, then grinned and

spat into the dirt. "You the button who's passing hisself off as Bad Bill?" he asked.

"Ain't he Longley?" Krag growled.

"He ain't."

There was a gasp from the watching men, all of them staring at the tall young Texan. Every man there was expecting the backing of the famous Bad Bill Longley, and this was not him.

"I'm not. But what I said still goes. You cut in, and so do I."

From the other end of town, a tall man, riding a huge blood-bay stallion, came slowly along the street. He saw the group outside the jail and knew from long experience what it meant. He also recognised one of the participants, and a smile came to his face.

"Waco, boy," he said softly as he halted the horse. "You've surely lost the bet."

Chándler looked at the group of men across the street, seeing they were wavering. He pushed home his point.

"Don't tell me they had you good folks thinking this here button was Bad Bill Longley?" he asked. "Waal, you're going to learn your lesson now."

The killer's hand went down in that flickering, lightning-fast move which had brought him through so many draw and shoot encounters. Too late, he realised that this was no dressed-up kid he was stacked against. Waco's hands went down just an instant after Chandler's draw started; but the matched staghorn-butted guns were clear and lined that brief, split-second ahead. The crash of the matched guns broke the silence of the street. Chandler pitched backwards, two holes in the centre of his chest and his wild-thrown shot crippling Brennan.

At the same moment, Krag fetched out his gun; but one of the men across the street brought up and fired his shotgun, and the gunhand went down into the dirt, a charge of buckshot teating through his vitals.

Waco holstered the guns and moved to one side. "This is between you and Walls, Duke."

A man leapt from the undertaker's shop, gun lifting. The rider of the blood-bay yelled: "*Waco*"—and a long-barrelled Colt came from his right holster to buck back against his palm.

Duke looked back and, as he did so, Walls made his move, hand dropping fast to the butt of his gun. "Duke!" Waco yelled.

Tavener came round, hand streaking down, but he knew that he would be too late. His hand gripped the gun, thumb starting to move for the hammer; but he clamped it down on the butt and brought the gun out. Walls's draw was fast at first, but he fumbled it— although he got the gun out and brought off the first shot. The bullet ripped Tavener's shirt and left a nasty burn on his arm. He steadied himself and his left hand came round to strike the hammer. The Colt bucked back, kicking high. Then it dropped into line again as he fanned the second shot. Walls reared back. He tried to line the gun as he went over, but his next shot went into the air. He hit the ground all spraddled out, arms thrown wide and the gun slipping from his lifeless hand.

"Good ole Duke!" one of the watching townsmen yelled. "We knew you could do it."

Waco ignored the people who came surging from the places where they'd concealed themselves to watch what happened. He went along the street fast, glanced down at the dead man and then up at the handsome blond giant on the blood-bay stallion. "*Gracias,* Mark!" he said and, drawing his right hand gun, kicked open the door of the undertaker's shop.

Mark Counter watched the young man, wondering why he was taking such caution. Waco went in fast, gun swinging in an arc; but the shop was empty, so he darted to the door at the rear. Flattening himself against the wall at the left of the door, he called: "All right,

Hodgkiss. Come out with your hands raised."

There was no reply from the other side of the door; so, carefully, Waco opened the door with a shove. He stood still, yet there was no sign of movement or anything else from the other side. Drawing his breath in, he hurled himself into the room, hitting the floor and rolling over. For an agonising moment he expected to feel lead smash into him. Then he came to his knees and looked round. The room was as empty as the shop, only the disturbed condition of it showing that Hodgkiss's departure had been fast. The undertaker knew that he would be the object of wrath for his part in this business, so had stayed not on the order of his going.

Crossing the yard, Waco opened the gate and looked out. The back street was almost devoid of life; but, in the distance, he heard the sound of a rapidly-departing horse.

"Lost something, boy?"

Waco turned and faced his pard, Mark Counter, who stood behind him, gun in hand. "Sure—nobody real important though."

Mark grinned. He watched with some approval the way Waco handled himself. It had been good to see the training instilled into the young man was being put to such good use.

"What's happening?" Mark inquired, as they walked back on to the main street again.

"Just ran into a mite of trouble," the youngster replied.

Before he could go further into the trouble, the cheering, yelling, excited crowd gathered round him. Duke Tavener and his wife were hugging each other and Banker Darcy came up with the other men of the crowd.

"Like to thank you for what you've done, Longley," the banker said.

"Longley?" Mark Counter looked at Waco. "What've you been telling these good folks, boy?"

Darcy stopped, his mouth dropping open. Then he

turned to old Amos Claypole. "You said he was Longley."

"Must have been mistook," the old-timer replied. "But it worked. You bunch were getting scared so I thought that, if you allowed Duke had backed down a man like Bad Bill Longley, you'd get your guts back again." He looked at Waco. "I didn't know Matt Chandler was in on this, or I wouldn't have risked getting you in deep. I knew you were a good hand with a gun. But I didn't know just *how* good."

"See?" Waco asked, looking round at the crowd. "You've got a real good lawman here with Duke, and you hadn't the guts to back him. You needed to think he'd got a top-gun to help him. If I was him, I'd be leaving this town."

Darcy nodded. "We deserve that. But I think I speak for the rest of us, Duke, when I say that I sincerely hope you'll forgive us. Hodgkiss put word out that you couldn't use a gun after you got caught out in the blue norther. Where is that sanctimonious——?"

"Gone, friend. Gone, and all but forgotten," Waco replied. "I aimed to ask him about the man who stayed here last night. Brennan. He tried to steal Pete Walls's gun back from the jail. Stayed in town all night, at the undertaker's shop. I went there and looked this morning, finding where his hoss was tied all night. From what I heard when I saw that *hombre* there"—he indicated Mark's victim—"with Hodgkiss, the undertaker, worked in cahoots with Walls. And Hodgkiss could have made the key that opened the jail safe."

Duke came through the crowd and asked the men to clear the street for him. When he was alone with Waco, he asked: "How did you know that I could handle Pete Walls?"

"Easy. Walls had been in the Territorial Pen for quite a few years. They let a man do a lot of things there, but they don't let him practise with a gun. I was on to it from the start. Why would Walls send word when he was coming, if he wasn't trying to get you on edge. And if you were so equal, he didn't need the edge. So I reckoned he must be right out of practise with a gun.''

Mark grinned at the young man again; he was proud of Waco's astute reasoning and knew Dusty would be too. Then he remembered something more important than pride in Waco's achievement.

''Boy, it looks like you've lost your part of the bet, too.''

CHAPTER THREE

Sam Ysabel's Son

The Ysabel Kid decided he was going to win the bet. It was a decision reached, not because he wanted the money, but for a desire to prove that he was a peace-loving man, sadly led astray by evil companions. He also was slightly suspicious that, when Waco cut the cards to decide the routes they took, the youngster had arranged that he, the Kid, should be sent into the one area where he was most likely to find trouble, the Rio Grande country.

The Kid halted his big white stallion in a wood overlooking the border town of Wet Slim. He swung down and led the horse out of sight into the wood, then set about making his preparations for avoiding trouble. Opening his bed-roll he took out a blue shirt and a pair of new levis trousers. Stripping off his all-black clothing, he changed into the other clothes, keeping only his boots, hat and black silk bandana. For a man who wanted peace badly, he retained his full armament. The gun-belt still supported the old, walnut-butted Colt Dragoon butt-forward at his right side and the ivory-hilted James Black bowie knife at the left. In the saddle-boot rested his magnificent One of a Thousand Winchester 73 rifle, something he would have felt lost without.

With his clothing changed he walked forward and strapped the bed-roll back to his cantle. Then, with an

Indian-like swing, he went up on to the horse from the right side. He sat there, his handsome, young and innocent-looking face with the red-hazel eyes impassive. Then he rode forward again on to the Wet Slim trail.

There was something wild and Indian about Sam Ysabel's son, Loncey Dalton. In his veins ran a blend of Irish, Kentucky, French Creole and Comanche blood; it made a dangerous kind of mixture.

The town of Wet Slim wasn't big; nor was it, particularly, a nice town. It existed to serve the needs of some five ranches bordering and surrounding it; and once was also the centre of a very flourishing smuggling gang. By some coincidence, when the Ysabel Kid left the area, the smuggling ended. His reason for coming here was to visit an old friend of his father; and to have a *pasear* along the river, to recapture memories of wild nights when old Sam Ysabel led his band over the water with contraband.

Yet, for a moment, the Kid was worried as he rode towards the only street Wet Slim boasted. The street was deserted; not a man stirred along it. Now the Kid knew that most of the citizens followed the ancient Spanish custom of siesta, but not at four o'clock in the afternoon. From the lack of visible life, he wondered if he was riding into a shooting. Then he saw the horses crowded in front of the Wet Slim saloon and the adjacent buildings, and knew that they would not be there if two men were going to face each other in a gunsmoke discussion. There was a lot of noise coming from the saloon, too—noise which might mean ranch crews in town for a celebration.

The big white came to a halt in front of a small, adobe-built establishment with a faded, weather and bullet-scarred sign in front, reading: *"Jock McKie, Fine Leatherwork."*

The Kid grinned as he slid from the back of his white stallion and left it standing untied in the shade around the side of the house. Jock McKie *did* make fine leatherwork; but his main sources of wealth once came from smuggled goods.

Walking as silently as a buck Comanche, the Kid went in front of the shop and opened the door. He came unnoticed, and at a very auspicious occasion, or he missed his guess, Jock McKie stood behind the counter, looking exactly the same as the last time when the Kid had seen him—like a sun-dried old banty cock. His hard, lined old face was bristling with aggression at the big, burly man with the low, tied gun of a practising gunfighter.

"And I'm telling ye that I'll nae gang, unless I feels like it?" McKie's Scottish accent improved as his temper rose.

"And I say you will," the man replied. "You get down to the saloon, like Mr. Handle wants."

"You tell Handle to go right straight to hell." McKie's accent was so thick that it could be cut with a knife.

"Yeah!" the big man reached out a hand.

There was a dry click and the man found himself looking into the worn bore of a Walker Colt, that looked as if it might have been one of the original Whitneyville thousand. Not that that detracted from its value as a deadly efficient weapon, and one which would do considerable damage at that range. The man took a step backwards, keeping his hand well clear of the butt of his low-tied gun—for Jock McKie was known to be able to call his shots with skill and accuracy.

"All right," he growled, trying to bluster his way out. "Don't come. Mr. Handle knows how to deal with that. You'll miss his trade." He turned and saw the Kid lounging by the door for the first time. He took in the old Dragoon, the cowhand dress and the innocent-appearing face—and made a mistake. "You!"

"Me?" There was a deceptive mildness in the Kid's soft-drawled reply.

"Yes—you. Get down to the saloon!"

"Says which?"

The big man's hand lifted to hover over the butt of his gun in a manner which often cowed young cowhands. "Says me."

The Kid straightened—and, suddenly, he looked as mean as two starving grizzlies with a Comanche Dog Soldier thrown in. "Suppose I tell you to go right straight out and climb up your thumb?"

"Bet you couldn't do it, Jacobs," McKie put in.

The man called Jacobs studied the Indian-dark face and tried to meet the red hazel eyes. Slowly his hand dropped to his side and he decided not to press the issue. This could have been due to a feeling of kindliness to the young man and general peace with the world. It could also have been because the lounging, innocent boy was suddenly replaced by as hard a looking *hombre* as it had ever been Jacob's privilege to look upon.

"Mr. Handle told me to collect everybody and take them down to the saloon," he said lamely. "He won't like it if you don't go."

"Leave us bow our heads for Mr. Handle. Whoever he might be," the Kid replied. "And you'd best collect yourself and go down there."

Jacobs walked towards the door; he heard Jock McKie's snigger, and decided to take his revenge at a more favourable time. He walked by the Kid and out of the shop, making sure that he kept his hand well clear of his gun. That boy there might look innocent, and might be wearing a gun that was long out-of-date, but there was nothing in his attitude to say he could not use the gun real well. There was also nothing in his attitude to make Jacobs believe he would regard any touching of gun-butts with anything other than dire suspicion.

"Howdy, Lon. Ain't seed you in a coon's age."

The Kid hid his disappointment. He'd hoped his change of clothes would be a good enough disguise to fool McKie. Yet here was the old feller holding out his hand and beaming fit to split his face from ear to ear. Taking the offered hand, the Kid remarked wryly: "I thought you wouldn't recognize me. How'd you know?"

"Take more than a change of clothes to fool me. You on the dodge?"

"Naw. And you look a damned sight older than when I saw you last. Place ain't changed none. Even got the same dust."

McKie grunted something about "damned fool sassenachs," then went on: "You came at the right time. Philo Handle's asking for real bad trouble. You don't know him. Bought ole Pan Briggs place. Pan was in a game one night, and thought two aces in his hand'd look better with the two he'd got hid out. Trouble war, the other gent held an ace up straight and after the shooting was over, the county sheriff sold Pan's spread for back taxes. Handle's niece from the East come out here to see him, and she's been kidnapped by Ramon Peraro. So now Handle's holding a meeting in the saloon, trying to get enough men together to pry her loose."

The Kid's returned lounging left him again. He leaned on the counter and his eyes bored into McKie's. "You mean he aims to go down into Mexico after Peraro and bring her out at gun-point?"

"Just that."

"The *loco bobo!* Don't he know about Peraro's way?"

"Naw. He's a dude. Jacobs is his manager and the rest of the crew are about the same kind. Can't see why some of them didn't warn him not to let the girl ride out alone. There's some of them you'll likely know. They all know Peraro's way all right."

"We'd best go to that meeting after all." the Kid growled.

There were few white men who understood, and knew, Mexico as well as this dark-faced young man. A whole lot of his childhood and early teens had been

spent in Mexico, and most of that time with the various
bandit gangs. He knew Peraro by reputation, and by actual contact. That girl would never be in more peril than
if any such attempt were made to rescue her.

The saloon was crowded with men from the local
ranches. They made a hard-looking crowd—for cowhands from along the Rio Grande acknowledged no
equals for salty toughness. The Ysabel Kid looked
round the room, trying to pick out anyone he knew.
Grange, the owner of the saloon, looked older and
fatter; but little else was changed—even the old band-
stand was still there.

Three men stood on the stand, one a fattish, short
dude with a florid face and thinning hair. The other two
were Jacobs and a rat-faced man in range clothes. The
Kid knew him to be a border-thief of the poorest kind, a
man neither his father nor any honest smuggler would
have any dealings with. However, the man, if he worked
for Handle, could have told the rancher of the danger
this plan held for the girl.

"I tell you they took my niece," the fat man was
yelling. "Those damned greasers came over the river
and kidnapped her. Took a white woman into their
stinking town and left a ransom note for me. Now I say
we should go down there and give those greasers a
lesson they'll never forget!"

The cowhands yelled their approval of his idea. They
were all angry at a white woman being treated in this
manner and out for revenge. Also, they saw their chance
of some excitement as a change from hard work on the
brush- and thorncovered range. The only faces which
did not show any eagerness to follow this plan were
owned by four well-dressed men who sat together. Two
he knew as the owners of ranches, the other two would
be the other owners. They were faced with losing nearly
all of their men for maybe a week; and also with the
prospect of serious trouble when the Mexican Government heard of an armed invasion of their country.

"Let's go down there!" a cowhand yelled.

"Hold it, gents!"

The Kid's words cut across the room and brought silence as every eye turned towards him. "What's all the trouble here?"

Philo Handle might be a dude, but he could tell that here was a fighting man the equal of any in this hard-case crowd. A man who would be a useful addition to his fighting force. "My niece has been kidnapped by a border rat called Peraro. He's asking thirty thousand dollars ransom for her. We intend to go down there and rescue her, then teach him a lesson he'll never forget."

"You could pay him," the Kid growled back, "and save some grief."

"*What?*" Handle screeched back.

"Pay him. If you can't afford that much, send word and he'll bring her back safe."

The crowd fell silent for they could tell that here was a man whom it would be trouble to cross. Handle alone spoke up: "Why should I pay him at all?"

"To get your gal back. What else did you figure on doing?"

"Taking every man who can handle a gun to Piente and bringing her back."

"Mister, that's plain, hawg-stupid. I know Peraro. He'll have his scouts out everywhere. Happen you'll fight your way to your niece. But you'll find her real dead when you get there."

"You know Peraro?" Handle could see some of the men wavering, so sought to discredit the young man who was standing against him. "That is a dangerous admission to make here."

The Kid pointed to the rat-faced man beside Handle. "Russel there knows Peraro, too——!" The man gave a snarl and his hand dropped.

The Kid's voice went hard and sharp as the bowie knife at his side. "Don't try it. You didn't have the guts last time, and you haven't now. I——"

A hand caught the Kid's arm and turned him as a voice growled: "All right, saddle-tramp. Get——"

The Kid's knee drove up savagely into the stomach of a burly, unshaven hardcase who had come up behind him and caught him by the arm. The man doubled over and the Kid's right hand twisted around, palm out, and brought up the old Dragoon gun to lay its four pound two ounces of solid weight hard on to the man's head, dropping him. Then the gun lined on Jacobs and the other—who'd once been known as Russel—as they moved forward.

"Mister!" The Ysabel Kid's voice was soft as a cooing dove, and as deceptive as the first gentle murmur of a Texas blue norther storm. "I know Peraro. So does Russel. Difference being that Russel worked for him one time, and could tell you plenty about him."

The rat-faced man looked pure murder at the Kid, but stood very still. Any man who called him "Russel" knew him well—far too well for safety. He did not yet recognize the Kid as a half-wild young savage who'd nearly slit his throat when Russel tried to bully him.

"Listen to this boy, you loco pack!" McKie bellowed. "He knows the border better than any of you. And I've tried to tell you that, if Peraro gets paid, he'll bring the gal back."

"Will the greaser play fair?" a rancher asked.

"Sure—that's the way he works," McKie answered. "Ward, you try and talk some sense into that bunch of your'n."

"Boys!" Handle roared. "All of you belly up to the bar and have a drink. Then we'll put it to the vote."

There was a wild rush for the bar in which neither McKie nor the Ysabel Kid joined. They watched in disgust, knowing that nothing they could say would change the minds of the young cowhands. Not one of that hardy bunch would have thought of going down there if they knew the risk and danger they were putting the girl in. They regarded this as a welcome relief from work, and a chance to fight the Mexicans; not as a serious business.

Ignoring the groaning man at his feet, the Kid walked from the saloon and McKie followed. He watched the young man, who was standing there looking at the horses with brooding attention.

"Got a knife, Jock?" he asked.

"Never without," McKie replied, reaching down and pulling a wicked-looking hunting knife from the top of his boot. "What the hell are you at?"

The Kid was cutting the reins of horse after horse, the eleven and a half inch, razor sharp bowie knife making nothing of the leather. "Never yet saw me a cowboy who'd walk, even to save a lady."

McKie grinned as he saw the Kid's plan. Then he asked: "What you fixing to do? Make like Georgie Washington and say 'I can't tell a lie, I turned your hosses loose?' "

"Nope. I'm going down there and try to pry her loose."

McKie stopped, his knife half-way through a rein. He was a noted poker-player; but, for once, he showed his surprise. Then he shook his head and severed the reins through. "Was it anybody but you, I'd say they was loco. Reckon you can do it?"

"Going to try. But I wish Dusty and Mark were here."

McKie knew why. The cowhands in the saloon would listen to either Dusty Fog or Mark Counter—for those pair were regarded as being the tophands in their line. The Kid, on the other hand, was noted more for his ability to ride scout, to follow a trail where even a buck Apache might fail, and to fight a Comanche Dog Soldier; but he was not regarded as a cowhand.

"Listen, Jock," the Kid said softly as they released the last horse. "I want you to get hold of all the ranch-owners, all but Handle. Tell them what I've got in mind. Tell some of the older hands that you can trust. Don't let out who I am to anyone. I don't figger anybody could get to Peraro before I do. But it won't help me any if he knows I'm the one whose against him. Something stinks about this whole thing. I want to get to the bottom of it.''

McKie agreed with this; and he was as wily an old border wolf who ever rode the dark trails and drove wet cattle or contraband over the Rio Grande. He also knew the task the Ysabel Kid was setting for himself and knew how little chance there was of it coming off. All the same, small though the chance was, if a man lived who could pull it off, Loncey Dalton Ysabel was that man.

The Kid whistled shrilly and his big white came from round the side of the shop at a fast run, sweeping along the street in a thunder of hooves. The Kid ran forward, caught the saddle-horn and went into the saddle with a single bound. In the same movement his old Dragoon gun came out and roared, and his wild Comanche war-whoop shattered the air.

The horses standing in front of the rails scattered all ways, breaking out and heading along the street, followed by the white stallion. The Kid swung over to hang over the flank of his horse, keeping it between him and the men who poured out of the saloon. Several of them held guns; but, before they could use the weapons, Jock McKie jumped into the trail in front of them, his old Walker Colt booming after the fast-departing rider. By the time this public-spirited action was over and the other men could manage to get clear, it was too late. The horses were streaming out on to the open range and the man was out of gunshot range.

''Who was it, McKie?'' a man yelled.

''Could have been a Mexican,'' McKie replied, ignoring the accusing looks.

Grumbling, the other man went along examining the cut reins, but one stayed back. He was a stocky, hard-looking cowhand, who rode as foreman for one of the spreads—a tough hombre, and an ex-Clay Allison rider.

He studied Jock McKie for a long moment, then re-marked:

"That yell sounded more Comanche than Mex. And that young heller in there looked real like a certain part-Comanche I knows."

"Sammywell," McKie looked piously to the heavens. "You are so right. You get your boss and the other three owners and come down to my shop. Don't you go telling Handle or his bunch though."

Holding the racing white stallion to a gallop, the Ysabel Kid left Wet Slim town behind him, driving most of the horses ahead of him. Then he cut the white off from after the others and watched the animals scattering. He was not worried that the men would lose their horses. A range-bred horse would always make for home if it was loose without a rider. It would take some time to round-up all the stock; and, long before that time was up, the Ysabel Kid hoped either to have rescued the girl, or to have met with an untimely end.

It was no easy task he was setting out on. That, the Ysabel Kid didn't need telling. He was going to need all his Indian savvy and more luck than any one man could rightly expect. Ramon Peraro was a powerful man in this section of Mexico. He was so powerful that not even Don Emilo Kosterliski's man-killing Rurales could get to him and end his promising career. However, there were three things Peraro needed to keep hold of his power. The first was the loyalty of his men, those hard, savage bandidos who would take any torture rather than talk. The second was his big black stallion, a horse which was, if not faster, at least the equal of the best the Rurales owned. The third, he needed two men badly to help rule his empire; these were Pedro Perez, his able second-in-command, and Jose Sanchos, the Alcalda of Piente. Perez was his shadow and made sure that no man ever got behind his back. Sanchos kept Piente safe for him, and warned of visits by persons of authority.

That was the only way to get at Peraro. He'd no kin

to be kidnapped, and would hardly have bothered if he had. But he needed those three, the two men and the horse. If they were taken, it would cost him heavily in both prestige with the other members of his gangs, and also in vital backing. The Kid hoped that he might get at least two of the three; and, if he were real lucky, he might even get all three.

All this the Ysabel Kid thought of as he rode along a narrow, winding trail through the thick brush of the Rio Grande. He rode without any apparent need to see where he was going, nor to study the occasional side trail. This was an old smuggler's route and one he could have followed just as well in the dark; in fact, he often had followed it in the dark. He came out on to the banks of the Rio Grande, the river which separated two countries. Up and downstream the Rio Grande ran fast, deep and treacherous; but, by some fresk of nature, it widened out here to make a gentle ford.

Easing the white into the water, the Ysabel Kid rode across the river, wetting up to the top of his high-heeled fancy-stitched boots. He was alert and his rifle came into his hand as the water lapped around the white stallion's legs. There might be a man or so watching this ford here, but it was highly doubtful. There were few enough who knew of the ford—which explained why it was not well used. The few who knew of it were border smugglers; and it was one of the few the American preventive officers did not know of.

For all of that, a man had crossed here a few days back—lone man riding at an easy pace. The Kid examined these tracks, but they meant nothing to him; not even when his tracks were joined by those of another who'd been waiting for him. The two sets joined yet two more men, who apparently stopped and talked together, then rode off. The Ysabel Kid made no attempt to examine the tracks further; they were of no interest to him and, as far as he could tell, bore no connection with Peraro.

"Tell you, Blackie hoss," he remarked. "Let's us look in on ole Juan Sebastion's place and say howdy."

The white went on at a steady walk through the bush, following a better-marked trail on this side of the river. It covered about a mile, when turning a corner the Kid found himself surrounded by grim-faced men, wearing dark grey uniforms and black braid down the legs of the tight trousers, and the eagle and snake badge of the *Guardia Rurale* on their high-crowned sombreros.

"Howdy, Don Emilo," the Kid greeted a tall, spare, handsome man who was wearing the same uniform, but in better quality material. "Remember me?"

Kosterliski, head of the Rurales, remembered the Kid well enough. He had good cause to remember—for the young man had helped him escape over the river when he was being hunted as a deserter by the American Cavalry. Also the Kid once helped him in a bit of trouble with a would-be revolutionary.

The face, with its short, pointed beard and small moustache, showed no expression for a moment. Then the firm white teeth gleamed, and he nodded:

"You are the Ysabel Kid?"

"Ain't but the one," the Kid replied modestly.

"I've heard it said that one was more than enough. Get down and eat with me."

It was more than a friendly request; it was an order, for Kosterliski was the law in the part of the land. The *Rurales* swung from their horses and soon two fine-looking coaches came rolling up. A camp was quickly set up and a good, cold meal laid out for Kosterliski and his guest.

"What happened to Duvalde?" the Kid asked after they'd eaten.

"Fell off his horse, poor chap, while we were fording a river. Drowned," Kosterliski replied cheerfully. "And now, what brings you to Mexico?"

"Peraro."

"The dear Ramon?" Kosterliski's face showed no expression. "And what has he done to attract the attention of the Ysabel Kid?"

The Kid wondered what Kosterliski was playing at. The head of the *Rurales* was the best informed man in the whole of Mexico and would be expected to know that Ramon Peraro was making a coup. However, there was little point in lying about it.

"Took a gal and brought her over the river."

"Are you sure it was Ramon? My pardon for appearing to doubt your word, but my information was that Ramon is having trouble with his men for not working. Why did he take the girl?"

"Ransom. He wants thirty thousand."

"Are her family rich?"

"Rich enough."

"Then you are taking the ransom?"

"Nope. Going to try to get her loose. Not for her kin—they don't even know I'm alive. What I don't figger is why they don't pay up. Got Russel riding for them and he knows Peraro, and what'll happen if they try and pry her loose. Aim to get a bunch of hands and come down here to rescue her. I tried to talk them out of it, but they wouldn't listen."

"They contemplate making an armed invasion of my country?" Kosterliski's eyes went hard.

"Did—but they won't for a piece yet," the Kid replied and explained why.

The Russian roared with laughter and slapped his thigh. "*Cabrito*, you are the most unusual man I ever saw. What do you intend to do?"

"Get her out of Piente."

"If any other man but *el Cabrito* said that to me, I would split my side in laughter. But with you I don't know at all."

"How do I stand with you?" the Kid inquired, knowing it would be best to put all his cards on the table.

"Meaning?"

"I just aim to bend the law a mite."

"In whay way?"

"First off, Colonel, I aim to kidnap Mexican citizens and tote them over the border."

"That is somewhat illegal, I've been told." Kosterliski watched the dark face all the time, knowing what the Kid had in mind. "If I was not going four miles up the Rio Grande, I might have to stop you!"

"Going to steal me a hoss, too."

"Dear me, is there no end to your evil-doing?"

"Happen I'll have to kill some Peraro's men while I'm doing it."

"Cabrito, I am a man of the law. Yet I am also a man who understands the necessity of such actions. I will carry on up the Rio Grande, and will not return for a week. By that time, you should have ended your business."

"I'll be riding then; I want to be in Piente soon after dark and it won't be long afore night now. See you, happen I make it."

"I hope you make it. Ramon is a thorn in my flesh, and I can't get near to him to remove it. Good luck, young man!"

"I'll likely need it," the Kid replied. He went to the big white stallion and swung into the saddle. *"Hasta le vista."*

Kosterliski turned on his heel and called to his men to prepare to move. He watched the young Texan riding off, a slim, lithe and strangely young-looking figure to be on so dangerous a mission. Yet the head of the *Rurales* doubted if any other man alive had even half as good a chance as the Ysabel Kid of succeeding.

The Ysabel Kid was worried as he rode up to and left his white at the water trough outside Juan Sebastion's *cantina.* The sun was setting, already, a few lights were lit inside the low, adobe-built establishment. There were several good horses tied outside the *cantina,* but the small front bar was deserted when the Kid came in. Only Juan Sebastion himself, big, fat and greasy as ever, was behind the bar. The Kid looked round; the room might be empty but there was loud talk from the other side of the thin wall.

Kosterliski should have known about the kidnapping, for he was the best-informed man in Mexico and very little happened that he did not know about. The Rurales would have spies in Peraro's gang, and yet they had not reported a very important piece of information like that. It almost looked as if Peraro and Perez were going to double-cross the other members of their gang. In that case, the chore might be some easier.

Juan Sebastion was a good judge of character and he knew this Indian dark young *gringo* spelled danger as he came across the room in silent steps. There was something familiar about the way this youngster moved, and the eyes; but Juan Sebastion could not be sure. He wondered if he should warn the men in the other room to lower their voices.

"Saludos, señor," Juan Sebastion began a welcoming speech in Spanish.

"Cut out that talk. I don't know it," the Kid replied in English.

Sebastion nodded politely, noting the butt-forward Dragoon gun and the knife. There had been one who carried such weapons, one who——

"I'll take me a drink," the Kid went on. Then, as Sebastion dropped his hand under the bar, he went on. "Knowed me a bar-tender who allus slipped something into a stranger's drink, just for laughs. He died real sudden when he tried it on a man who knowed the game."

Sebastion spoke very good English, despite his lack of culture; he knew exactly what his customer meant, and did not like the implication. He also changed his plan and left a certain small, green-coloured bottle lying where it was until some less suspicious caller came.

"I say Ramon is wrong!" a voice yelled from the other room and, although it was in Spanish, the Ysabel Kid understood it perfectly. "He says we must hide here for another few weeks and it is long since we last made any money.''

"Softly, fool! If one of Ramon's friends was to hear you it would go hard on all of us.''

"It might,'' the first voice replied, still loudly. "I, Paco Santovel, am not afraid of Peraro, nor of Perez. Sebastion! More wine for my friends.''

Sebastion picked up another bottle and crossed the room, passed through the door and closed it behind him. The Kid went cat-footed to the wall and listened to the conversation, which suddenly dropped to almost whispers.

"What kind of a man?''

"Young, but bad, Paco. Much like *el Cabrito.*''

"*El Cabrito?*'' Santovel's voice rose slightly. "Is it he?''

"No!'' There was scorn in Sebastion's voice. "This one can't speak Spanish—and *el Cabrito* spoke it as well as we do.''

The Kid returned to the bar and lounged there; he'd finished his drink when Sebastion returned and now leaned there as if he'd never moved. He set his hat right on his head, turned and walked out. He mounted the big white and rode from the *cantina,* into the fast-fading dusk. He was thinking again; here was proof that at least one part of the Peraro bunch did not know their leader was holding a girl for ransom. It smelled like a big double-cross and, given luck in getting hold of at least two of three things he wanted, the Kid would be in a position to dicker.

The town of Piente was built in a circle, with the Cantina del Peraro right in the centre of the protective shelter. To get to it, a man would need to go right between the other houses where every man was Peraro's ally. The Kid knew Piente well enough, although he'd not been there for several years. Like an Indian, he possessed the rare faculty of retaining a map of any place he visited in his head.

Leaving the big stallion without saddle or bridle, on the banks of a stream, the Kid faded into the blackness and through the street of the town. Most of the houses were dark and deserted-looking, but from a few came sounds of revelry. The Alcade's office was beside the jail; a look though the window showed this exalted official in his full glory.

Sanchos lay in comfort on a soft couch. He was a fat, bloated man wearing silver-filigreed clothes, his bare feet sticking out from the end of the trousers, the fat toes wriggling as he thought over his many blessings. For an obscure official in the Government at Mexico City, Sanchos considered he'd come far. He was Alcade of a thriving town, and drew revenue from various sources which would hardly have met with the approval of *el Presidente*. Of course, to a man with money, there was no reeason why *el Presidente* should ever know. That was why Sanchos was so valuable to Ramon Peraro. The fat man knew the right people in Mexico City; and, from them, in return for certain monetary favours, he got much information.

The Alcade was a dreamer. Lying back on his comfortable couch, he dreamed of what he would do ith the ransom money when the *gringo* girl's relatives paid for her safe return. He also dreamed what might happen if the other members of the gang found out Peraro and Perez intended to double-cross them and not make a fair share-out. This latter dream disturbed him, and he tried to refocus his mind on the pleasures he would be able to buy in Mexico City with his share.

"Señor! I have need of your help, *señor,"* a whining voice said from outside the door. It was the voice of a poor peasant, requesting help from an important official. "My wife beats me and has driven me from my home."

Sanchos bellowed a curse back: *"Vamos,* you swine! How dare you disturb your Alcade when he is resting, for such a small thing."

"She is not small, *señor*. She is very big and fat. Also, she hits me with a broom, *señor.* "

Sanchos came off his couch and caught up the silver-engraved riding-quirt from the desk. It was a present from Peraro and very handy in quelling his *peons,* when they became annoying. He crossed the room and flung open the door, ready to inflict another beating upon this whining *peon*. However, he could see nothing and stepped out of the doorway. A hand shot out of the blackness, gripped Sanchos' shirt and hauled him away from the light. The hand then gripped the greasy black hair and dragged the head back. A razor-sharp knife rested against Sanchos' fat throat.

"Silence, or I will remove your head." The voice was still speaking in Spanish but was now low, hard and savage.

The *Alcalde* was an arrant coward and went limp, his legs shaking under him as he croaked, "Please *señor,* do not do this evil thing."

"All right, but we will take a walk from this place. We will walk as friends and, when we pass anyone, you will remain silent. If you wish to shout a warning to them, you may. But, if you do, the mission bells will toll requiem and you will not be hearing them."

Sanchos was blubbering with fear as he walked out and along the street. The quirt was removed from his sweating and tight-clenched hand by this savage-talking, yet silent-moving stranger. In fact, there were times when Sanchos wondered if he was still escorted, or if the man from the night was just a figment of his *tequila*-loaded imagination. He was coming to a well-lit house, from which sounded shouts and laughter. For a brief instant, he considered shouting for help; then something sharp pricked through his shirt, in a gentle warning to him.

Not a word was spoken as they passed through the houses and out into the open range country. Sanchos shuddered, wondering why this man by his side wanted him—and what the reason he had for bringing so important a friend of Ramon Peraro away from the safety of Piente Town?

"We will speak softly," the voice went on in his ear. "How many men know of the *gringo* girl?"

Sanchos gulped; he wondered if the man was one of the other gang members who'd found out about the double-cross. "Peraro, Perez and I," he replied. "Don Ramon held a *fiesta* and a grande *baile* on the day he brought her into town. None know she is held at his house."

The Ysabel Kid nodded to himself, his suspicion confirmed. Peraro was aiming to double-cross his other men on this kidnapping. That made things some easier; the bandit leader could hardly call on his men for help, without admitting he was trying to do them down.

A low snort came from the blackness of the woods, and Sanchos almost screamed as a huge white stallion loomed from the darkness. The Kid forced Sanchos nearer and hissed, "I am *el Cabrito*. You guessed that?" It was satisfying to see that, even after an absence of several years, his name still held its magic below the border. "You know my horse? He will watch you and, if you try to escape, will kill you. Where is the girl, and who guards her?"

"At Don Ramon's house—and, tonight, he guards her."

"And Perez?"

"He drinks at the house of Rosita Phillipe. He is very angry, for men have left town when they should not."

The *Alcade* felt his hands pulled behind him and a cord passed round them. He realised that, to perform the tying, his captor must no longer be holding a drawn weapon. This gave him comfort, for he was not a fighting man. Not for him the sudden attack which would render his captor helpless. He knew any attempt at a sudden attack would meet with an even more sudden, and extremely painful, defence.

The Ysabel Kid did a very good job of tying the *Alcade*, bringing the fat man down hard to the ground and leaving him lying there helpless. He stepped back and looked over his handiwork, then remarked:

"I leave you now, *senor*. Pray that no one comes to your aid. If they do, you will die. My horse will see to that."

Sanchos shuddered and mumbled incoherently through the gag the Kid had forced between his lips. He rolled on to his back and twisted his neck round. The big stallion loomed up in the darkness, but there was no sign of the Ysabel Kid. He was gone in complete silence.

On his way back to town, the Kid wondered if he could get into the Peraro place and get the girl out without fooling about any more. He doubted it; Ramon Peraro was no fool and kept efficient sentries around his place; he also kept a couple of very fierce dogs in the grounds. One mistake there, and the girl would die a painful death. That was Peraro's way. If the ransom was paid, he returned his captive promptly unharmed and usually with a present or two. If there was any attempt at rescue, the captive was killed without any mercy. It was by sticking to this code that Peraro obtained payment whenever he held anyone to ransom.

The Ysabel Kid knew that, and so did Russel.

So this time the Kid's direction was not towards a house, but to the rear of the Peraro *cantina*. In the stable at the back was Peraro's black stallion, held there under constant guard, ready for his use. This time the Kid's knife was out and ready. It boded ill for any man who crossed his path, for the Kid had little respect for human life. Less when opposed by these savage, almost inhuman killers who rode for Peraro. He was willing to kill if need be, and only kept the Alcade alive for use as a hostage. The Kid intended to play the game as Peraro wanted; if the bandit kept his side of it, so would Loncey Dalton Ysabel.

The guard at the stable door was asleep, lying flat on

the ground, head resting against the wall. The Kid moved closer, silently, the knife held hip-high and ready to use. He knew the man would be a light sleeper; to sleep while guarding the horse he would need to be. If Peraro found him asleep, the sentry would most likely wake up in a far hotter climate.

The sentry's eyes opened and he started to come up, hand fanning towards his belt. The Kid lunged in, his foot driving up in between the man's legs. stifling with numbing agony the cry he was about to give. Then the bowie knife made a flicker of silver in the darkness, its point biting into flesh and the razor-edge cutting as it enlarged the opening. The body heaved convulsively, a low moan bubbling through the lips. Then it was still.

The Kid came up to his feet, rubbed the blade of his knife clean on the man's serape. He heard footsteps approaching, and faded into the blackness, hugging the side of the shed.

"Jose, you dog!" a voice grated. "Where are you"

The Kid stood silent, heart beating faster and the tension mounting in him. He knew that voice. Pedro Perez was coming towards him.

A stocky wide-shouldered man came out of the blackness, staggering slightly like he'd taken too much *tequila*. This did not fool the kid, for Perez had a reputation of being more dangerous drunk than sober. Then the Kid remembered that, at night, either Peraro or Perez always checked on the sentries guarding the horse.

Perez halted and looked down at the still form on the ground. He came closer and snarled: "So. I've caught you asleep at last, have I? Do you think, because you are a friend of Santovel, that you will escape punishment?"

Reeling forward, Perez smashed a kick into the still shape on the ground. Then he bent over and put his hand down. He must have placed it right on the wound, for he jerked it back with a muffled curse. Too late, he

heard a soft sound and started to straighten up. The Kid
moved forward and, having substituted his Dragoon
gun for the knife, brought it down on to Perez's head,
dropping the man as if he'd been poleaxed.

Opening the stable door, the Kid dragged Perez in. A
small lantern was burning in the building and, in the
light, the Kid saw Peraro's black stallion in a stall. A
second horse was in another stall. The Kid glanced at it,
then ignored it—until he remembered he would need a
mount for the *Alcalde*.

Throwing a saddle on the black, the Kid worked fast.
He fastened Perez's hands and feet together, then
checked to make sure there was no danger of the man
recovering before they left town. With a strength that
seemed out of keeping with his lithe figure, the Kid
hoisted Perez across the saddle and lashed him there.
The Mexican would be uncomfortable, but the Kid was
not worried about that. In his time, Perez had made
more than one man and women even less comfortable,
so he could expect little pity from the Ysabel Kid.

With the second horse saddled, the Kid took time out
to write a note to Peraro. He led the two horses out into
the night and, taking the knife from the dead guard's
belt, pinned the paper to the door, leaving Perez's guns
and the *Alcalde's* quirt lying under it. Then he mounted
the second horse and, leading the black, rode out of the
town. He kept to the main street and rode in plain view
of everyone who might be looking—for, in a town like
Piente, travellers often waited until the dark hours
before starting a journey, but they did not sneak out by
the back ways. To do so would invite closer inspection
than a bold ride out through the main street.

At this time of the morning, the Kid guessed most
people would be either drunk, or asleep, and he was not
unduly bothered when he got clear of the town. He did
not waste any time in idle speculation of his luck.
Collecting the still-terrified *Alcalde,* he pushed on north
to the border, crossing it as dawn broke the sky. This

time, he pushed into the deep brush country again, riding along a narrow trail which brought curses of pain from the now-conscious Perez.

The white stallion stopped and the Ysabel Kid's old Dragoon gun slid into his hand. "Come on out!" he said.

"Danged if that hoss ain't part hound-dawg, the way he smells out a man!" McKie replied, as he stepped from the bush.

The Kid accepted this tribute to his stallion's prowess, and then said: "How did you figure on this place?"

"Know you. I figgered you'd come here as being the best place to handle any business."

The old-timer turned and walked back by the way he'd come, and the Ysabel Kid followed him. They came to a clearing, or rather a small basin in the bush country; the slopes were gentle and the bottom about a hundred yards square. All round the basin, except for the two openings, one each side, the scrub and bush were thick and all but impenetrable for a man. However, they did not stay in the clearing, but rode straight across and up the other side. Then the Kid swung down from his white and helped McKie get Perez down from the horse and fasten him to a tree. The old-timer gripped Perez's nose and held it until his mouth opened, then inserted a bandana as a gag. The *Alcalde* was not fastened nor gagged; there was little danger from him in either way. He was too scared to attempt yelling warnings; and, with bare feet, not even a buck Apache could walk through this thorn bush country.

The Kid was not finished yet. He took McKie's horse as being fresher than the others and turned his white loose to forage. Mounting, he looked down at McKie. "I'm just heading back to the ford, to wait. I want to see if Peraro is followed."

"You don't allow he'll come alone?" McKie scoffed.

"Sure, he will. None of the others in his bunch know he's got the girl. But he just might be followed.

Santovel and some of the others don't like the way he's
been doing things.''

The Kid took a roundabout route through the bush
and reached the ford from a different direction. He hid
the horse, praying that it would keep quiet. Then, with
his rifle in his hands, he slipped into the bush and lay
concealed, waiting.

Ramon Peraro looked around the now-silent *cantina*
with disgust. His men were all drunkenly asleep, lying
on the floor, or across the tables. He rose and crossed
the room, a tall, lithe man wearing expensive, silver-
decorated clothes and belting a silver-mounted Colt in
an ornate holster at his right side and an ivory-handled
finely-chased knife at the left. His face was fattening
now, but still handsome, the eyes hard and cold.

He was almost at the door, meaning to go to his
room, when he realised that Perez was not back from in-
specting the horse. A suspicion came to him. Perez had
taken a fancy to the *gringo* girl and might be with her,
trying to force his attentions upon her. Peraro was not
averse to such things—and, if the ransom was not paid,
would have given his consent—but he would not allow it
before the appointed time of payment came round.

He stamped out of the *cantina*. Then he stopped, staring at the open stable door and the still shape illumi-
nated by the lamp. Anger filled him that a member
of his gang would so flout his authority by sleeping,
when he should be guarding. Peraro crossed the space
fast; he was still some distance away, when he realised
that the guard must be dead. He knew the man as an in-
veterate sleeper on duty; but one who could sleep so
lightly that approaching him and catching him were next
to impossible.

Stepping over the body as of no consequence, Peraro
entered the stable and a savage curse broke from his
lips. The two stalls were empty; both his prized black
and another good horse he'd stolen recently had gone.

Peraro spun round on his heel, intending to rouse his men and scour the country around for the thief. Then he saw the guns and quirt on the floor and the knife-pinned message on the door. With a savage hand, he tore the paper down and held it in the light, so that he could read it.

"Peraro,"—the writing was sprawling and awkward—"I am writing this in English so none of your bunch can read it, if they find it first. Bring the gringo girl across the Rio Grande to the place where Tortilla used to meet the arms-seller. I have Perez, the Alcalde and your two hosses. A fair swap."

There was no signature, but Peraro had not been expecting one. He stood silently in the night, an angry snarl on his lips. Then, slowly, he took out a match and lit it, burning the paper and crumbling the ashes. There was no doubt about one thing: he must take the girl back. The gang were getting restless—and, already, Santovel was growing too big for his breeches. Without Perez to back him, Peraro knew he could not long hold down the other members of the gang. Nor could he handle the ransom of the girl alone; and, if the gang discovered her, they would demand revenge.

It was still dark enough for him to collect the girl and get her out of town without being seen. He went to his house and woke the Indian woman who was lying on the floor, telling her to collect two horses for him. Then he went upstairs and knocked on a door. After knocking twice, he heard sounds of a bed creaking and a female voice asked, in English: "Who is it?"

"Peraro, *señora*. Prepare yourself to leave."

The door opened and a pretty, freckled faced girl with long red hair looked out. She was sleepy-eyed and yawned. She looked at him dazedly. "What did you say?" she asked.

"You are free to go. I will escort you to a place where a friend will be waiting to take you home."

It took a moment or two for this to sink in. Then she

opened the door fully. She was wearing a rumpled blouse and divided skirt just as she'd worn when caught; for Mavis Handle had not undressed since she was first brought there. She was a sensible girl and knew that, although she'd been treated well enough and respectfully by her captors, they were two of the most dangerous men in Mexico. All too well she knew that the kindness would end abruptly enough if she disobeyed them in any way.

"Has Uncle Philo paid?" she asked.

"He has sent for you."

"If he's paid, I'll bet he's died of heart failure," the girl stated. "He was never so fond of me, he'd pay to get me back again."

"Come, please!" Peraro was getting impatient.

The Indian woman was waiting with two saddled horses when Peraro and Mavis went downstairs. They collected the horses and rode out of town, heading for the Rio Grande and the same smuggler-crossing the Ysabel Kid had used earlier on. Peraro ordered the girl to keep quiet until they were well away from town. However, once they were clear, he allowed her to talk. The sun was coming up now, and, as they rode along in the fast-coming daylight, Mavis asked: "You got your money?"

"You are free, are you not, *señora*. Your uncle would have been wise to pay."

The girl smiled and shook her head; she wondered why he was showing so much caution as he rode along.

"My Uncle Philo would hardly pay to get me back—not under the present circumstances. He's too fond of the dollar; and there is another reason he would rather I didn't come back," she replied. "I thought he would rather let me die than pay."

Peraro glanced sideways at the girl. "That was not what Russel told me when he came to make the arrangements for kidnapping you."

"Russel?" she frowned. "Who is this Russel?"

"A border thief, not one of the best. It was he who set you up for this." Peraro knew that he could never let the girl and her rescuer live, and so talked to her. "I was never really happy about it. When I offered him too small a sum for his share, he accepted it without argument."

The girl did not know anyone called Russel and so did not connect the name with her uncle. She watched the Mexican as he lapsed into silence, then wondered why he was telling her all this.

They reached the Rio Grande and crossed by the ford; the girl was a good rider, and made the crossing with ease. She followed Peraro on to the other bank and, although they passed within a few feet of him, neither knew they had a watcher.

The Ysabel Kid watched them go by; he could have dropped Peraro there and then, but would not do such a thing. If Peraro played fair, so would the Ysabel Kid.

The Kid stayed on, lying under the bush and watching the river for a time; he was trying to gauge it correctly to arrive at the basin before Peraro brought the girl there. When he was satisfied that Peraro really was alone, the Kid turned back and collected his horse. He put his spurs to work and let the animal gallop. He rode like a centaur through the bush country and along the narrow, winding trail, coming to a halt at the top of the basin.

"He's coming, Jock!"

"Alone—and with the gal?"

"Sure. Perez and Ramon aimed to double-cross the others in the bunch," the Kid replied, taking off his belt and removing the knife from it. He pushed the sheathed bowie knife into his waistband at the back, making sure it was not in sight. Then he strapped on his gun-belt again.

Peraro rode down the slope and halted at the edge of the open ground. He shouted, "*Hola, señor.* I have the girl here."

The Kid vaulted into the saddle of McKie's horse and

rode into view and, for the first time, Peraro saw his opponent in this desperate game. The Mexican frowned as he studied the dark-faced young man on the other side of the basin. There was something familiar, and yet unfamiliar, about the *gringo*. Peraro tried to think who this man was. What one lone man could have entered his town like that and kidnapped Perez, the *Alcalde* and taken the two horses. All too well, Peraro knew how light a sleeper the sentry was, yet he'd let this man get near enough to die before he woke properly. The kidnapping of the *Alcalde* would not be hard, but Perez was another proposition. The bandit was far more dangerous drunk than sober, and he would be a veritable *tigre* to catch.

Peraro thought of all the deadly men along the border, trying to decide which of them might be capable of this. None of them fitted the bill; for none of them would even bother to rescue the *gringo* girl. Strangely, he did not think of *el Cabrito*—for it was several years since the Ysabel Kid rode the Rio Grande.

"Leave your weapons up there, and I'll leave mine this side," the Kid called back.

Peraro dismounted and drew the rifle from his saddle-boot, watching the *gringo* repeat this. Then he unstrapped his gunbelt but, in putting it down, slid the knife from its sheath and shoved it into the top of his boot. The move was very smoothly done and Mavis, so intent on watching her rescuer, did not notice it.

The Kid collected the reins of the two horses and led them out. Perez was still gagged, and the *Alcalde* tied to his mount to prevent him from falling off. The small procession moved down the slope and Peraro came forward, leading the girl.

They halted and left the horses, coming together on foot, the girl following Peraro and wondering who this dark, handsome youngster was. He looked far too young to be doing anything like this.

Peraro, too, was studying the Ysabel Kid, from his

pushed-back JB Stetson and the curly black hair to the
high-heeled boots on his feet. If the Kid had been wearing his usual clothes, Peraro would have recognised
him immediately and acted in a far different manner. As
it was, the Mexican decided to kill this young upstart.
These *gringos* were all alike; guns were their weapons.
None of them appreciated the value of a knife as a
fighting weapon.

"Who are you, *señor?*" he asked.

"I didn't ask you that," the Kid replied in English,
knowing that his Spanish might give him away. "I've
returned your men, and you've brought the gal. I'll take
her back to her ranch and I reckon you'll leave her
alone."

Peraro smiled mockingly. The young *gringo* stood
with his hands behind his back, thumbs hooked into his
waistband. He was in a perfect position for a killing
slash.

"You may think what you wish, *señor!*" he
replied—and lunged forward, with the knife coming
from his boot-top and driving up at the Ysabel Kid's
body.

The girl screamed as she saw the knife, thinking that
such speed must take her rescuer unaware. She reckoned
without all the long years of training, and the Ysabel
Kid's Comanche-wild co-ordination of mind and mus-
cle. Even as Peraro's knife reached out for his vitals, the
Kid side-stepped and the eleven-and-a-half-inch blade
of his bowie knife glinted in the sun. Peraro's blade was
parried and pushed aside. The Kid's knife ripped in low.

Peraro nearly died at that moment. His lunge, aimed
at what should have been an unsuspecting and un-
prepared man, was sent with all his strength. The knife
blow missing, caught him off balance and, just in time,
he saw the bowie knife coming up at him. Flinging himself to one side, he felt the blade of the other's knife just
touch him. He whirled and crouched, the knife moving
in small circles as he attacked.

"I never saw a *gringo* who could use a knife," Peraro
hissed, as he slashed at the lithe shape before him.

The Kid avoided the ripping cut with a bull-fighter's
grace and cut in, bringing the bowie knife up in a savage
drive. "You never heard of James Bowie?"

The men circled, knives leaping and flashing in the
sun. The true knife-fighter always went for the stomach
first, the throat as a next resort; never for any place
where he could only hit bone and do little perma-
nent damage. These two were good, very good. Perez
watched, and then threw a leg over his saddle-horn, to
jump down. Although his hands were tied, he came
towards the Kid, launching a kick at him.

It was desperate now; and the Kid knew it. He
avoided the kick and almost ran into a knife-thrust,
then jumped clear. Fighting a man like Peraro was
dangerous enough, for the Mexican was skilled with his
knife; and, with this added edge, he could write finish to
the Kid.

Perez lowered his shoulder and tried to charge the
Kid. At the same moment, Peraro lunged in and the Kid
gave a shrill whistle. Jumping back, the Kid slipped on
the grass and went down. The girl screamed in terror.
Peraro yelled in triumph. Then hooves thundered and
the fighting scream of a stallion, awesome and terrible,
shattered the air as the huge white stallion came racing
down the slope.

Perez prepared to leap in at the *gringo* boy who'd
shamed him when he heard the hooves and turned to see
the huge horse rearing above him. He twisted aside,
trying to avoid the iron-shod hooves. Then the white
killer-horse was upon him, screaming, stamping and
biting. Mavis Handle screamed again. She saw old Jock
McKie, from Wet Slim, running down the slope. Then
her knees gave way and she slipped to the ground in a
faint.

Peraro hurled forward, his knife lashing down at the
young man. He came close, very close, to doing what

several other eager and aspiring gentlemen had tried to do. The Ysabel Kid rolled over, the knife missed his arm, but ripped the shirt-sleeve to the wrist, pinning it to the ground. Unfortunately for Peraro, it was the wrong sleeve and the bowie knife ripped up. Once again, the Kid felt the puff of hot fetid air rush against his hand, and knew his knife was buried in the other man's stomach.

Rolling the body from him, the Kid got to his feet, drew out the knife and rubbed the blade clean on the ground. "You allus was a hawg, Ramon," he said. "I'd have played fair, if you did."

Then the Kid heard Jock McKie's scared shouts and turned his attention to his big white stallion. Perez was down and, although he never looked much in life, made an even worse picture in death. The stallion in its fighting rage had almost kicked Perez to pieces. The Kid, Indian callous as ever, just grunted, then snapped: "Ease off there, Blackie!"

The wild fury left the stallion's eyes and it backed away, snorting loudly. The Ysabel Kid went up and calmed the big white, patting its neck and talking to it. He saw McKie bend over the girl and asked: "Is she all right?"

"Just fainted, I reckon. That hoss of your'n nigh on made me faint when he went for Perez."

"Take her up the slope. I'll attend to this down here," the Kid replied.

Jock McKie helped the girl to her feet and, shielding her from the bloody sight of Perez's shattered body, led her up the slope. The Kid turned on his heel and looked at the terrified *Alcalde*.

"Your patron is dead. Don Emilo Kosterliski is up-stream there; if you take the bodies to him he may go easy on you. Then you can do what you want to."

"*Si, señor.*" The *Alcalde* was shaking, but also working out what his chances of survival would be if he went back to Piente and word got out what happened here in Texas. The time was on hand for a patriotic *Alcalde* to declare to the forces of law and order that his town was infested with *bandidos*. Kosterliski would be pleased with that.

On an impulse, after he'd loaded the bodies on to the two horses, the Kid asked: "Have you seen Russel lately?"

"He saw Don Ramon a few weeks back, and again more recently. I think he was the one who told us where to find the girl."

The Kid was thoughtful as he went up the slope, watching Sanchos riding back towards the border and leading the Peraro horses. The girl was sitting on a fallen tree-trunk and looked up at him. Despite her face being a trifle pale, she was well on the way to recovering her poise again.

"I'd like to thank you for saving me," she said.

The Kid grinned modestly, as if rescuing girls was an everyday thing in his life. "Sorry you had to see what you did," he replied. "You'd best get some rest, ma'am. Then we'll take you back to Wet Slim."

"Got me some food cached back there a piece— figgered you might need it," McKie put in.

The Kid grinned as he rose. A man could always trust Jock McKie to do the right thing, even without telling. The old-timer's food cache proved to be a fair feed, and by a stream of clear water. The Kid left the others to go upstream, taking his black clothing with him. He returned washed, shaved and attired as he usually was, all in black. The girl, looking at him, thought he was not more than sixteen. She could hardly reconcile this inno-cent-looking youngster with the savage, unshaven knife-wielder who had battled to save her life.

They settled down to eat the food McKie had brought out from town. The old-timer looked across at the Kid. "You riled a tolerable heap of folks, scattering the hosses that way. I thought Handle would be fit to be tied."

The girl frowned. "I can't see Uncle Philo going to all that trouble just to save me."

"You stop them coming?" the Kid ignored the girl's remark.

"Nope. I talked to some of the ranchers, and to Sam Walton. Told them what you said. Sam's the man the cowhands foller. Nice gent—but a mite too fast with a gun for comfort."

"Know Sam all right. He used to ride for Allison's CA. He'd want to lend a hand when he knew."

"Sure did," McKie grunted. "I talked him into staying in town and riding with the bunch that's going down there today."

"Today!" the Kid snapped. "How about hosses for them?"

"Handle sent over to his spread for the remuda. They should be in town now and the bunch starting out."

Mavis shook her head. "I can't believe it. Uncle Philo actually going to all that trouble, and risking riding to my rescue."

"Reckon so ma'am?" the Kid asked.

"I know so. It would be the other way about, if anything. I'd have thought, what with one thing and another, he'd have taken this as a heavensent opportunity to get rid of me."

The Kid watched the cynical twist of the girl's lips and knew she was telling him the truth. Certain suspicions started to form, or to crystallize, now. He bent forward eagerly. "You reckon your uncle might not want you to come back?"

Her face flushed red as she realised that she'd been giving this young Texan a close look at a very dark family skeleton. "Well, I may have been hard on poor uncle Philo. I could have judged him harshly. After all, he was gathering men to come and rescue me. He couldn't have——"

"He could, and did," the Kid replied, his face tense now as he watched the girl. "If he'd come down there after you, Peraro would've killed you.''

"Would Uncle Philo know that?'' she asked.

"He'd got at least one man riding for him who did—Russel.''

"Russel?'' Her brow puckered in a frown. "Peraro talked about him. I don't know him and, to the best of my knowledge, we never hired a man called Russel.''

"Name's Jones now,'' McKie put in.

"Jones?'' she gasped out. "He was the man who suggested that I should ride out along the Rio Grande the day I was kidnapped. I wanted to do some painting, and he told me a place where I might find some rattlesnakes. I wanted to paint them.''

"You found the rattlers all right, ma'am—as dangerous a bunch as you could,'' the Ysabel Kid growled. "I'll see Russel when we get back to Wet Slim.''

Listening to that soft-drawled, gentle voice the girl could not restrain a shudder—for she knew the meeting would be very painful for the man this black-dressed cowboy saw.

"Do you know,'' she put in, "I still don't know who you are?''

"The name is Loncey Dalton Ysabel,'' he replied. "You maybe heard of me more as the Ysabel Kid?''

Mavis stared at this dark-faced boy. She'd not been long in the south-west but, in that time, she's heard much about the Ysabel Kid. All of what she'd seen him do today went far towards making her think it was all true.

"What did you mean about Uncle Philo getting me killed?''

"That's the way the Peraro bunch worked,'' the Kid replied. " 'Bout four years ago, to take just one case, Don Figaro Coronado's gal was kidnapped by Peraro's bunch. The ransom asked wasn't large; ole Ramon always asked reasonable. But the Coronado's are a dead mean bunch, and didn't want to waste good money. They tried to force their way into town and cut down

Peraro's crowd. They were whip-sawed from the start to the end, there being a rifle behind every wall. Held the Coronado's fifty *vaqueros* back easy and bust Don Figaro's shoulder. What was left of the *vaqueros* started to tote him back, when Peraro shouted: 'Here's your gal,' and sent her out across the back of a hoss.''

"How?"

The Kid looked the girl up and down for a moment. "Just think about the worst thing a man could do to a pretty, innocent convent gal. Double it and you won't near have reached the answer. See, ma'am, Peraro's got him a reputation. He kidnaps somebody and, like you saw, treats them real well. I bet you never been treated so politely. Then, when the ransom note is met, he sent them back. Took the daughter of one of my friends below the border. When he was paid, he gave her a silver bracelet that would have cost, maybe, a thousand dollars if he'd bought it. Sent her back in his own coach. But if he doesn't get paid off dead on time—or someone tries to rescue the prisoner—he kills and he doesn't kill nice.''

"So you think the Uncle knew about this?"

"Couldn't help but know. Russel must've been working for him," McKie snapped. "Don't you reckon so, Lon?"

"It figgers. Russel knows Peraro's way; he was in Piente when the Coronado gal got hers. So, if he'd set you up for Peraro, he'd warn your Uncle about it. If he war working with Peraro, that is. He wouldn't get paid until after the ransom money was delivered, so he'd surely warn your uncle. Wouldn't want you killing. That means he went along with this, knowing what would happen to you.''

"Uncle Philo can be pretty persuasive when he likes," Mavis replied. "I would think it was his idea from start to finish. He particularly needs me out of the way now.''

"You like to tell us, it won't go any further," the Kid

remarked. "Might make it easier for us when we get back to Wet Slim. Specially after what I did before I left."

The girl listened to how the Kid had prevented the previous day's rescue attempt. She was even more impressed by the casual way he talked of it, knowing that he could easily have been shot down for even trying it.

"I'll try and square things up for you when we get back. I don't think there will be any trouble over it, and I'll see any horses which are permanently lost get paid for. But, about Uncle Philo—well, he needed me out of the way. He is only my manager. My father controlled the money in our family; he had a knack of making it. Land speculation, mines, cotton, he was in them all, and Lucky Jack Handle always came out winning. Most of his money came down to me when he died. Until I reach twenty-one next birthday, Uncle Philo is in charge—although I'm afraid Papa didn't trust Uncle Philo, for he made sure that very little of the actual money came his way. This ranch was just another venture, but I found that money was being diverted into it at a rate which the return didn't warrant. That was why I came here and I saw that I'd made a mistake in coming. Uncle Philo was all smiles and friendliness, which in itself should have warned me. He told me Jones—or Russel, as you call him—would show me round. I think he must have considered various ways of getting rid of me."

"Russel would help some," the Kid remarked. "I know him. If you should've gone under, who would get your money?"

"Uncle Philo and two other relations back East," she replied. "I'm afraid that my father's lawyers will remove Uncle Phil from control. They've been trying to for several years now. I wouldn't let them; always felt sorry for him, I suppose."

"Do you now?" the Kid asked softly.

"Not any more."

"Good."

There was something in the way he said it made her look up hard at him. The face suddenly was no longer young. It was hard, cold and expressionless, yet, in those red-hazel eyes, she read finish for her uncle, unless something happened to save him. The face held her attention; it wasn't innocent now. She could not place where she'd seen that expressionless mask; then it came back to her—a painting of a Comanche warrior. The face of that brave was exactly the same as this Indian dark boy's.

"Lon," she looked at him. "I—er—I——"

"You'd best get some rest. Then we'll ride back a piece and see what we can do."

The girl suddenly felt very tired; she was only too pleased to relax on the Ysabel Kid's bedroll while he flung himself down on the ground and went to sleep. For a time she lay watching him. Then sleep came over her. Jock McKie rested his back against the tree and, with a rifle across his knees, kept watch.

"Time to move, Miss Mavis," McKie said as he shook the girl's shoulder.

She sat up and looked round. The sun was high in the sky, and she got up. The Ysabel Kid sat with his back against a tree; he was whistling and cleaning a magnificent rifle. Rising, he crossed to her. She looked at the silver plate in the butt, reading the inscription on it:

"Presented to Loncey Dalton Ysabel.
FIRST PRIZE, Rifle Shoot, Cochise County Fair."

The girl looked up at her rescuer from the rifle. She wondered if he was the same man; that innocent, baby face was there again and the pleasant, even smile on it.

"Time we went," the Kid remarked.

McKie brought her the horse she'd ridden from Piente and she mounted, then waited until the Kid collected his big stallion and rode back. "We'll head along the river for a piece, and try to stop them fools crossing over into Mexico. If they go over the line, there'll be all hell to pay."

Neither Mavis nor McKie thought to argue with the Ysabel Kid on this, in view of his capable handling of the situation so far. They followed him and Mavis became probably the first woman ever to see the winding smuggler trails through the thick bush of the banks of the Rio Grande. She wondered how many men could remember the many turns and twists but the Ysabel Kid never even hesitated.

At last, he drew up his horse in the bush at the side of a large, well-marked trail. Although she could never have told how they came to be there, she recognized this piece of trail as being just above the main ford to Mexico. She wondered why they waited, then heard the rumble of many hooves. Shortly after that, the Kid pointed, and she saw men coming into view. They were mostly cowhands; but she recognized that fat shape of her uncle at the head of the party, flanked by Jacobs, Russel and another of his men.

The Kid wanted the men alongside before he made a move. He sat still, with his rifle across his saddle. Unfortunately, he hadn't told Mavis this and, before he could stop her she'd ridden out, calling: "Hello, Uncle Philo!"

Philo Handle's hand went down. For a fat man he moved real fast and the bullet tore Mavis's hat from her head. Before he could draw a fresh line on the girl the flat bark of a rifle shattered the air. Philo Handle slammed backwards from his saddle, his gun falling into the dirt.

"It's a trap!" Jacobs yelled, snatching at his gun.

Sam Walton, the man who'd been suspicious in Wet Slim, brought out his gun and smashed it down on to Jacobs' head, knocking him from his horse. At the same moment, Russel was covered by another of the party.

"Hold it, all of you!" the Kid roared from the bush. "I'm coming out."

Walton grinned at the Indian-dark youngster and jerked a thumb towards Jacobs and Russel. "Real trigger-happy bunch, ain't they?"

"Sure. Man'd say they wanted Miz Handle dead, not rescued."

The other men gathered round—the younger hands looking in awe at a man who was no older than themselves, but who was a legend in his own lifetime. Now he wore his usual clothing; they guessed at his identity and most all of them guessed right.

Mavis slid from her horse and went to bend over her uncle. He lay in the trail, blood pumping from the wound. Slowly, his eyes went to her and he gasped: "Your father's luck rubbed off on you, girl."

"Don't talk, Uncle Philo!" Mavis replied. "We'll get a doctor for you."

"Do you think it would be any use?" Handle croaked back at her. "I know I'm done for, and it probably is as well. It was a good idea."

The girl straightened up. She heard a gasping rattle and blood gushed from her uncle's lips. When she looked down again, it was all over. The Ysabel Kid was right; her uncle would never trouble her again. She felt her legs shaking and a hand caught her arm. She looked round at the Ysabel Kid. For a moment, she didn't speak. Then she gasped: "Take me home."

The Kid told McKie to ride with the girl, and several of the hands agreed to go along. Then, after they'd gone, Walton looked at Jacob and Russel, who were huddled together under the guns of the rest of the party. The ranch-foreman grunted as he watched their scared faces.

"What we going to do with them, Lon?" he asked.

"Leave it to you. But Russel set her up for Peraro to kidnap—knowing that, when the boys here tried to rescue her, she'd be killed."

"He did that?" Walton growled; and through the crowd went a savage rumble—for, in the West, not even horse-stealing was as severely dealt with as harming or endangering a good woman.

"Sure," the Kid replied. He explained the way Peraro worked and what he'd found out.

At the end of the recital, Walton looked around the crowd, then back at the Ysabel Kid. Next, he asked a question that was on the mind of every man in this crowd: "What'll we do with this bunch?"

The Kid swung into the saddle of his white again after getting down to talk to the men. He looked back, his face innocent and his voice gentle. "Why Sam, didn't your mother never tell you nothing at all?"

He turned the horse and rode back towards Wet Slim, while the cowhands formed a circle round the two scared men. Two ropes were unstrapped from saddlehorns and put to the appropriate use.

The Ysabel Kid joined up with Mark Counter, Waco and Red Blaze in Bennet City. He'd spent a pleasant week at the Handle ranch, helping to get Mavis' affairs there straightened out. The girl was selling the ranch and going back East again; there were too many unpleasant memories for her to want to stay.

The four young men rode out of Bennet together, headed on their way towards Tensonville and the last member of the bunch. The Kid rode his white by Mark's side. He chuckled as he looked at the tall, handsome man.

"Wall, it looks like I lost out. How about you?"

"Me?" Mark replied. "I had a time, Lon. A real time."

"How about the bet?"

"Reckon I lost it, too."

CHAPTER FOUR

The Major

Mark Counter walked into the town of Casa Grande. He was carrying his saddle and bed-roll slung over his shoulder, and letting his limping blood-bay stallion follow him. The usual dandified appearance Mark presented was absent this time—after two wet and miserable nights sleeping out in the open. His expensive white JB Stetson hat with the silver-concha-decorated band was splashed with mud; although like a good Stetson, it still held its shape. His face was unshaven, the almost classically handsome features marred by a two-day stubble. His clothes gave little indication of their expensive cut, and his high-heeled, fancy stitched boots were well smothered in mud. Only the brown, hand-tooled Joe Gayline gun-belt around his waist—with the matched brace of ivory-handled Colt Cavalry Peacemakers, tied low—was clean. A man kept his gun clean at all times in the West. If he was a careful man, he did; and Mark Counter was very careful.

Mark wasn't in a very amiable mood; never being one to relish the pleasures of outdoor life, he had just been forced to spend two nights sleeping out on the rain-drenched range. If his horse hadn't picked up a stone bruise, he could have spent each night in comfort.

Casa Grande was changed since the last time he came through it. Word was that a railroad branch line was coming this way; so folks from the East, ever eager to get in on any boom, rushed west to buy up land and build a town. So Casa Grande spread out to twice its old size and more. Yet it was strangely quiet for a boom-town; the street, at this early afternoon time, should have been filled with wild crowds, pushing, shoving, headed to and from the various saloons. The scene here was one of peace—the sort of peace only a real good lawman could bring to a wild wide open township.

The Casa Grande Hotel was the first place he saw; yet even that was changed from the last time he'd seen it. Then it was a drab-looking, none-to-clean place owned by an old drunk. Now, it was painted up on the outside and clean curtains were at every window. They were en-couraging signs. Mark walked slowly towards the build-ing, deciding to sleep there. If the inside was as clean as the outside, it must have changed hands—for the last owner was said never to have any trouble evicting unde-sirable guests. The bed-bugs would pick the undesirable up and throw him out of the window.

A man came from the fence-walled side of the corral and through the gate, leading a team of the sorriest, sore-backed, harness-galled mules it had ever been Mark's privilege to witness. The man leading the mules was tall, not quite up to Mark's three inch over the six foot level. His shoulders were as broad as Mark's but without that graceful tapering to the hips of the hand-some young Texas giant. In dress, he might have been anything; the check shirt was tucked into levis, which in turn were rammed, hit or miss, into heavy boots. The whip in his hand, taken together with the sorry mules, gave the true clue to his business. He was a mule-skinner and this was his team.

Mark frowned as he looked the animals over; they were in no shape to be worked, but the big black-haired and dark-chinned man did not look like the sort to let that bother him. However, it was nothing to do with Mark, and the code of the West did not allow for chance interference in another man's actions. Not unless the interferer aimed to back his play with either fists, or a smoking .45. Not that Mark was afraid to back any play he made with either. His reputation as a fighting man was high—and it would have been far higher, if his capacity for such was not always dimmed by his riding under the shadow of the Rio Hondo gun-wizard, Dusty Fog. But there was the bet to think of and, unless the man actually ill-treated the mules in front of Mark, there was nothing the Texan could do about it.

"Blue, Big Blue!" a woman's voice snapped out. "You're not using that team."

The woman stepped into view as she spoke, the words being backed by a double click as she worked the lever of the Winchester rifle in her hands. The mule-skinner half-turned and looked along the barrel of the rifle as it lined full on him. His hard face twisted into an ugly snarl, while his hand hefted that coiled whip as if he aimed to use it on the woman.

"They're my team," the man growled back and across the street. Mark Counter relaxed. He'd been ready to take a hand if the mule-skinner used his whip on the woman, but there was no danger of that now. When the man started to talk, Mark knew there was no danger of him doing more than talk.

"That's right." The woman's rifle never wavered. "And so are all the other mules at your camp. I took this lot to care for them, and I don't aim to have you abusing them any more. Get down to your camp and pull out with another team. You can collect these when they're better."

For a long moment the pair looked at each other. Then, snarling under his breath, the mule-skinner let loose of the lead mule and turned to walk away. He stopped and looked back at the woman as she led the mules back to the corral, shook his fist after her and snarled: "One of these days I'll be back to see you for this."

Mark watched the man walk away, then shrugged; it

was nothing to him. He led the horse through the gate
and followed the woman round the side of the hotel to
where there were three corrals laid out. She turned the
mules loose into one of them, then turned and gave her
attention to him.

For the first time, Mark really looked her over. She
was tall, five-foot-eight at least, in her flat-heeled shoes.
Her hair was black as a raven's wing, the deep blackness
that shone almost blue. Her face, framed by the long
hair, showed signs of real beauty, rich, full and mature.
Her figure, in the tight-fitting gingham dress, was
buxom and shapely; the dress clung to it in a way that
showed she was wearing little more than the dress. He
guessed her age was around forty; yet she was well-
preserved in this harsh land which dealt roughly with
beautiful women.

Standing with her strong-looking hands on her hips,
the rifle leaning on the corral side behind her, she asked:
"Have you seen my husband?"

"No, ma'am. Can't say I know——"

"He's down at that Iris Pendleton's place again,
that's where he is. Don't you deny it. You men are all
alike—a fat blonde strumpet comes to town and, right
away, you all forget you've got wives and homes."

"Waal, ma'am, I'd——" Mark tried to get a word or
two in but she was not even listening to him.

"Don't argue with me. I know her kind. I bet she got
turned out of the last town she was in, and now she's
trying her games here. I'll stop her, you see if I don't."

"Likely ma'am. But, right now, I'm more interested
in getting a change of clothes, a bath and a shave, then
sleeping in a real comfortable bed again."

The woman stopped talking and looked him over.
This unkempt saddle-tramp was speaking with the accent of a cultured southern gentleman. Her eyes bored
through the mud and dirt and recognized the costly
clothing of the young Texan. Then her gaze flickered to
the horse and she snapped: "Have you ridden him?"

"Not for two days, ma'am. He picked up a stone bruise a couple of days out and I walked since then."

She went out and talked soothingly to the big stallion, bent down to examine the injured leg. She straightened up and nodded. "Stone bruise. He'll be all right with a few days' rest. Have you carried that saddle for two days?"

"Sure, didn't want to put any more strain on the leg than was necessary. I could surely use that bath, ma'am."

"Come on in then—after you've put your horse in a stall. If you can't afford it, I'll find you work around town until the horse is better."

"I'm not near the blanket yet, ma'am, thank you. Reckon I can manage to stay on here for a spell."

With his horse in a loose stall and contentedly munching at the hay in a net on the wall, Mark turned his thoughts to his own comfort. He followed the woman into the hotel through the rear door. The inside was just as clean as the outside showed, the floor carpets swept and the ledges around the walls dusted. They went along a passage and into the entrance hall. This was deserted, the register open on the desk top. The hall was small. A set of stairs leading up to the first floor were at one side; the other opened on to a bar which was, strangely for a town like this, empty.

Mark signed in the register, then followed the woman upstairs. She opened the door of a small room and allowed him to enter, carrying the saddle over his shoulder. He put it down on its side and looked round the room. The bed was clean, the sheets white and fresh-looking. A small table and chair were against one wall, a washstand at the other. He went to the open windows; they let on to a balcony, which looked down on the corrals. It was a neat and pleasant room, of a far better standard of cleanliness than was usual in a small-town hotel.

"Get those clothes off. Leave them here and I'll have

them washed for you, Mr. Counter,'' the woman ordered. "I'll fix the bath for you right now.''

Mark's war-bag, in his bedroll, yielded a complete
change of clothing for him. He selected a tan shirt,
tailored for him and a pair of clean levis. Then with his
clean socks and underclothes under his arm, he went
along to the bathroom. He was pleased to get out of the
dirty gear and hand it round the door to the waiting
woman. Then he sank into the luxury of a hot bath.

It was some time before Mark returned to his room,
clean and once more looking his normal self. His hat lay
on a hook behind the door, cleaned of all the mud and
marks of the past few days, but his boots were nowhere
in sight. His gun-belt lay where he'd left it on the bed,
and he was pleased to see that the woman had not
touched it. Pulling on a pair of plain moccasins, Mark
slung the gun-belt round his waist and left the room.
The hall was deserted, but there was the sound of
someone moving round in the bar. Mark walked into
the room and looked round. The tables were set out and
the chairs which had been on top of the tables were now
round them. A man rose from behind the bar. Mark
went across towards him, but was not looking at him;
his full attention was being directed to the full-length
painting on the wall behind the man.

The painting was of the woman, when she'd been
somewhat younger. She certainly was a beauty then, the
years had dealt kindly with her. She stood with an old
model Navy Colt in her right hand, wearing a Union
Army Major's coat and kepi. Below the bottom of the
coat, she wore nothing but black stockings and high
boots. The legs were curved, shapely and attractive.
Beneath the picture was a well-shone brass plate on
which was engraved: *Major Pauline Cushman, Scout of
the Cumberland.*

"Man—so that's who she is!" he said.

The man behind the bar nodded. He was a tall,
darkly-handsome man, a town dandy and a lady-killer,

Mark guessed. His clothes were expensively cut and he wore them well.

"That is Pauline Cushman Fryer, friend. I'm her husband: Jere's the name."

Mark took the proffered hand; it was the grip of a professional hand-shaker. Jere Fryer was a man with charm, and he knew it, he was the sort who would likely wind up as a political sheriff of some county. Yet he must have something, if a woman like Pauline Cushman had married him.

"Name's Mark Counter," Mark introduced, then went on: "I've heard some of Pauline Cushman. She was quite a gal."

"*Was?*" Fryer hid his pleasure at meeting so well-known a man, with an eloquent wave of his hand to the picture. "She still is. I married her right after the war. We were in the same theatrical troupe. Did you hear about how she was the Union's top spy in the War?"

Mark had heard of Pauline Cushman, but was not willing to concede that her efforts made any great difference to the running of the war; not as much as the spying of the Confederate ladies, Belle Boyd and Rose Greenhow, anyway. Yet the woman they called the Scout of the Cumberland made some little name for herself.

Fryer poured out two drinks, without asking what Mark fancied, and set them up on the bar. "Did you hear how she fought and licked the Confederate spy, Belle Boyd, in the Elite Theatre?" he asked proudly, though both he and Mark knew this was distending the truth. Pauline did fight with a Confederate sympathiser in the Elite Theatre, Louisville. But the other woman was not Belle Boyd; and the fight ended in a draw, when the star of the show, enraged at losing the limelight, banged their heads together, putting both girls out. Fryer knew the true facts; but saying it was Belle Boyd made a better story.

"Never did hear that one," Mark replied; as a stout

Confederate, he was not willing to concede that any
Yankee could lick a reb at anything.

Jere Fryer pushed out his chest proudly; it was plain
to Mark that whatever suspicions Pauline Cushman
nursed about her husband, the man was genuinely
proud of her. "After the war we toured the country.
Then, when we'd made enough, she bought this place.
You may know what it was like before. Well, she turned
everyone out and scrubbed it from top to bottom. Then
we got it fitted up properly. That was before the town
boomed wide open. When it did, Pauline said she
wasn't having any wild and wide-open stuff here. We
couldn't get a marshal and, after she started, we never
did need one. She surely held this town down. Like the
time two of the local ranchers looked like starting a
range war here. She got them and made them shoot it
out in the street here—and wouldn't let any of their men
join in. Price took lead, but he finished Johnson. Then
Pauline laid Johnson out and patched Price up."

"Surely runs the town," Mark remarked.

"She sure does." Fryer warmed to his subject, and
went on eagerly: "Take the madame of that cat-house
on Back Street. She used to cuss so loud that the local
ladies didn't dast walk anywhere near the place. So
Pauline went and asked her to quit it. The Madame got
sassy and they fought for near on an hour. But after the
licking she got, the madame don't cuss any more. Then
there was a big German gal who did most of the washing
in town. Wouldn't do it clean, and used to go round
dirtying anybody's who did their own. Pauline went to
see her. Man, you've never seen so much hair flying in
all your life; but that German gal sure does the wash
good now. That Pauline's quite a gal—quite a gal!'

The door of the bar-room was thrown open and
Pauline Cushman came in. Three or four thin-faced,
sniggering women watched from the door of the hotel.

"Jere Fryer. I've warned you about going to see that
slut, Iris Pendleton. You stay away from her."

"I only went to see if she'd like some help with her hotel——" Fryer started to object.

"Hotel, is it?" Pauline snapped back. "You mean a cathouse. And she's as bad as that fat female mac on Back Street."

Mark walked across the room and from the bar. He went upstairs, hearing Pauline Cushman telling her husband in no uncertain terms what she thought of the fat blonde who'd be better off on Red Light Street, San Francisco, than here among decent, ordinary folks. Mark carried on upstairs, other people's domestic troubles both bored him and made him feel uncomfortable. He could quite well see Jere Fryer showing any pretty young woman attention, even though Fryer did have a wife as beautiful as Pauline Cushman. At the top of the stairs, Mark turned; the townswomen were still listening; but, even as he watched, they turned and hurried from the hotel to make their way along the street, calling out to other women as they passed.

Mark went into his room and removed his gun-belt. He sat on the bed and took the cleaning gear from his war-bag. He cleaned the two guns and his rifle, then lay back on his bed and went to sleep. He lay back in comfort, eyes closed for some time. Then the door of his room burst open. Mark came off his bed with a lithe bound, his right-hand gun lining and the hammer easing back under his thumb.

Jere Fryer halted; several other men behind him also stopping as the handsome blond giant came up with his gun ready for use. Fryer gulped, then said: "Easy now, friend. I didn't know this room was being used. The boys and I want to use the balcony. Iris Pendleton's coming after a showdown with Pauline, and the Major's out in the corral."

The men didn't wait for further invitation, but trooped by Mark and made for the window. With one exception, they were the sort of men Mark would expect to be Fryer's friends. Fairly well off men of the town, owners of small businesses; or, maybe, working at the bank. The last man in was a slim, elegant-looking gambler dressed to the latest height of frontier gambling fashion. His cut-away coat was light grey, with darker facing on the collar, his shirt frilly-bosomed and the string-tie immaculate. His trousers were tight-legged and almost white, the shoes under the trousers shining enough to reflect the sun. To ordinary eyes, the man was not armed; but, to Mark's experienced gaze, that slight bulge under the left arm spelled a shoulder-clip with a short-barrelled weapon in it.

Mark watched the men troop through, then put the revolver back into its holster and followed them out. Looking down, he saw Pauline Cushman in the corral, and realised, from her general relaxed, watchful attitude, that she was not unaware of Mrs. Pendleton's coming. She ignored the crowd of people who were standing all round the corral, treating them as if they were not there at all. Up on the balcony, Mark watched this crowd and guessed that near every man and woman who could walk was there. He saw a big, red-faced, red-handed woman with long blonde hair and guessed that she was the German washerwoman who didn't clean the clothes until forced to by Pauline Cushman. Further along, separate from the good ladies of the town, and among a bunch of grinning, loud-talking cowhands, stood a short, heavily-built woman—who, by dress and general appearance, must be the madame of the local cat-house.

Mark frowned, he was no moralist and wouldn't want to set up as a pious do-good man. He liked his entertainment frontier style, wild, woolly and uncurried; yet there was something about this spectacle below that sickened him. The crowd were watching with a kind of drooling expectation. They were watching to see two women fight with each other, and they were hoping Pauline Cushman would be beaten.

A rumble of expectation ran through the crowd, and

one of the watchers on the balcony pointed excitedly down to where a woman was coming through the crowd. She walked through the gate of the corral and advanced on Pauline Cushman. Up above, Jere Fryer grinned delightedly at Mark. "That's Iris Pendleton!"

Mark studied the young woman and wondered if he'd over-estimated Jere Fryer. Iris Pendleton was a tall, buxom young woman; but although she was good-looking in a cheerful, open way, she was nowhere near the woman Pauline Cushman was. Her blonde hair showed from under the ribbons and cover of her sun-bonnet. She wore a tight-fitting old gingham dress which clung to her large, swelling bust and was tight around her firm waist, then over the swell of her hips and flared out to leave her legs free. She looked a pleasant, cheerful young woman, if one not overful of moral scruples. She was plainly the sort who would enjoy the company of men without ever thinking of preying on them.

"Tell you she's at least ten pound heavier than the Major," one of the loafers said. "And taller."

"All right then, Jere!" The gambler became brisk and businesslike. "You want to bet me five thousand your missus wins?"

"Certainly, Dud," Fryer replied eagerly.

"I know you're good for it, but I want paying today."

For a moment Fryer looked worried; then he studied the two women, who were now standing face-to-face below. He laughed and held out his hand. "Bet!"

"Bet," Dudley Fellowes, owner of the .45 Saloon, replied.

In the corral, Pauline Cushman and Iris Pendleton faced each other. They looked like two cats on a fence. It was the blonde girl who spoke first:

"I hear you've been talking big about me."

Pauline looked the blonde girl up and down with magnificent disdain. Then, with a contemptuous, though theatrical, shrug, she replied, "So you're Mrs. Pendleton? I rather expected something like you."

"You did, did you?" Iris's voice rose a shade as her temper flared up. "Listen, you fat old hag——!"

"I haven't time to listen to every cheap harridan who comes here," Pauline replied. "I thought Jere had better taste."

Iris's breath hissed out in a savage rush. She clenched her right fist and swung it. The fist crashed against the side of Pauline's face in a punch that sent the older woman crashing to her back and brought a rumble of delight from the crowd. Pauline landed hard, but she came up with a bound that would have done credit to a much younger woman. Her left swung, the solid smack of the blow sending echoes back from the confining walls of the buildings round the corral. Iris went crashing into the corral fence, clinging there and, as Pauline rushed at her, smashed a left into the Major's eye.

They hurled at each other like two enraged wild-cats, hands driving into hair, tearing and tugging, as they spun round screaming, kicking, scratching and punching. Then they crashed to the ground and rolled over and over in a flurry of wild, waving legs and flailing arms. There were no rules in such a fight as this— anything went; and it would be far worse than two men, for the women were insensible to pain or mercy—like two primeval jungle creatures each trying to savage the other.

Iris got the first advantage; Pauline was on her back and Iris threw a shapely white leg across the Major's straining, heaving body and sat on her, driving savage fists into her face and head. Pauline gasped, arching her back and heaving the younger woman over. Then, as Iris landed on hands and knees, she shot out a grasping hand to grip the back of her frock neck and claw the other into the blonde hair, ripping the sun-bonnet clear. Iris screamed in fury as she struggled to get free of the grip which left her with no chance of defence. It would have gone hard for her if the old gingham dress, not meant to stand such treatment, had not torn. The ripping sound was loud and the cloth split to the waist. Iris pulled forward, twisting round to meet Pauline's attack and disregarding the fact that her dress slipped down off her shoulders. She tore free of it and went down with Pauline on top of her, completely oblivious of the fact that she was now naked to the waist and her large, full breasts were exposed to the view of the watching crowd.

Over and over they thrashed on the ground, first one then the other on top as Iris's tearing hands clawed Pauline naked to the waist. The crowd were wild with excitement, screaming advice to the fighters and yelling the support and approval to whoever they favoured.

"Tear her hair out, Iris!" the fat German washer-woman screamed.

"Smash her teeth in, blondie!" the brothel's madame howled.

"Kick her! Stomp her!" yet another woman whom Pauline had snubbed on some occasion yelled, forgetting that she was supposed to be a lady.

To give Iris her due, she was trying to oblige all of the other women. One hand tore at Pauline as the Major lay under her, the other smashed into Pauline's face, while Iris's feet hacked and kicked at the other woman. Then Pauline threw Iris off and she got up. Her frock was ripped to the hip by then, and her black stockings were burst through at the knee; one had come loose from under the garter and now hung around her ankle.

Iris also rose, sobbing for breath, and attacked again. Both women had lost their shoes; their skirts were ripped; and each had blood flowing from her nostrils; both showed the start of a mouse under at least one eye. Pauline swung a savage punch and they stood toe-to-toe, smashing home blows like two men. Then they closed again to fight with tooth, feet, knees and other brutal and savage female styles of defence. The fight raged from one end of the corral to the other, without a let-up. They were exhausted, sobbing for breath; yet neither would give in.

Then Pauline was knocked to the ground by a wicked upper-cut, which brought her down hard. She lay there dazed, and feeling as if every inch of her aching, pain-wracked body was on fire. Through the spinning haze, she saw Iris loom above her and, in that moment, realised how young the blonde was. She saw the shapely, smooth white leg emerge from the torn slit of the dress and noticed that, unlike her own knees, it could be exposed to view without needing stockings to cover the harshness long hours of scrubbing had left on Pauline's. Next, the Major's eyes went up over the tattered frock to the smooth, heaving and dirty, yet still-firm stomach. For a buxom young woman, Iris showed no fat. Her waist was trim, widening out to round, full breasts—which stood out like white mounds in the same way Pauline's once stood as she posed in a *risqué* tableau as Aphrodite rising from the waves.

In that moment, Pauline realised her own age and felt scared for the first time in her life. She saw the blonde's foot lift to stamp on her, and sheer instinct came to her rescue. Her hands shot up, catching the foot. Then she lunged into a sitting position, carried it to her mouth and bit the toes—hard.

Iris screamed as the pain knifed through her. She lost her balance and crashed to the ground. For all of that, she was up again and, with a scream which was more animal than human, threw herself at Pauline in an attack that made the earlier stage of the fight look gentle. The older woman was driven back as the savage onslaught sent her reeling; slaps, kicks, punches rained on her and her own defence grew more weak. Driven the length of the corral and back, Pauline stumbled blindly before Iris, sobbing and almost helpless.

Upon the balcony, Mark Counter watched with growing disgust. The other men were screaming for

Pauline to end the fight; but Mark knew she was beaten
and it was only a matter of seconds before Pauline
Cushman's reign in this town was over. Mark was a
fighting man, and he had seen many fights between both
men and women; yet never before was there one so
savage and brutal as this. His every instinct told him he
should go down there and separate the two women; but
he knew that the man who did would have to face that
screaming, jeering mob who were now swarming over
the corral rails to get a better view of the end of the
fight.

Even as Mark decided to end the fight, and left his
room, Pauline was sent down by a wild haymaker that
caught her under the jaw. She lay on the ground, sobbing, being unable to force her pain-racked body to do
anything but try to draw air into her aching lungs
through her battered mouth and nose. She could hardly
see and the roaring in her head only let through one
sound—the jeers of the women as they encouraged Iris
to batter her still more.

Iris stood over Pauline for a moment, swaying and
hardly able to keep her feet. Then she bent and scooped
the other woman up by the hair. Pauline's legs looked
like two heat-buckled candles and would not support
her, but Iris was not done. With a snarl of hatred, she
drove her right fist into Pauline's stomach in a brutal
and damaging blow which doubled the other woman
over. Her other fist came up; it caught Pauline under
the chin and lifted the older woman erect, then right
over on to her back.

"Give her some more, Iris!" a woman screamed.

Staggering and almost falling, Iris knotted her hand
into Pauline's hair and pulled her head up, then
smashed a punch into the battered, bloody and dirty
face. It was the last thing Iris was capable of; her hands
lost their grip and she went to her knees, sobbing in
pain, while the crowd swarmed round her, cheering and
yelling.

The town photographer, a short, fat man—who was sweating profusely and almost drooling with the sensual pleasure of what he'd witnessed—shoved forward, carrying his camera. "Stand with one foot on her, Mrs. Pendleton!" he suggested eagerly.

Iris looked round her. Her breasts heaved and she sobbed breath into her lungs. Her face was marked by the fight, both eyes blackened, the nose, lips and cheeks bloody. For the first time, she seemed to realise how she was attired. With a gasp, she tried to cover her breasts with her hands. Then she gripped the tattered side of Pauline's frock and pulled. Pauline's limp figure rolled over as the frock was torn from her, leaving her lying with nothing but a pair of long-legged knickers, one tattered stocking and a garter. The blonde was helped to her feet by women who, until then, wouldn't even have spoken to her. They wrapped the torn frock round her shoulders. The madame from the house came up with a handful of Pauline's black hair which she'd gathered from around the corral.

"Here, blondie," she said, forcing it into Iris's hand. "Something to remember this by."

Iris stared around. Then she gave a half-scream of pain and embarrassment and shoved through the crowd. They followed her, cheering and yelling delightedly—leaving Pauline Cushman laying in the corral, a battered, forlorn and unconscious heap.

The photographer looked round; there was no one about. He focused his camera and took one photograph of Pauline lying there. Then he moved round to get another exposure. They would sell well; he might even be able to sell them to some Eastern newspaper. It was a pity that cameras would not take moving photographs. A set of pictures from the fight would have been something, and would have made the fortune of the man who took them.

He was too busy with the camera to hear or see

anything and, as he ducked under the sheet for the focus, felt a hand grip the slack of his trousers. He gave a startled yell as he was hauled out from under the sheet, then another hand gripped him by the scruff of the neck. The photographer was lifted as if he was a baby; he saw the scene spin round and was facing the corral rails; then was pushed towards them and lifted. He yelled as he sailed over to fall into the horse-trough at the other side. By the time he'd shaken the water from his eyes, he found himself looking up at a handsome blond giant, who was eyeing him with a very disapproving look.

"Did you get any pictures?" Mark Counter asked grimly.

"No, mister, none," the man lied.

"Mister, happen you did get any, I wouldn't print them. If you do, and I hear about it, I'll come down here and tear you limb-from-limb."

Saying this, Mark turned on his heel, opened the rail-gate of the corral and went to Pauline. She still wasn't moving and he bent down to lift her as gently as if she'd been a baby. He held the limp, dirty and battered body in his arms and walked back into the hotel, carrying her upstairs to her room. Inside, he lay her on the bed and looked down at her. Then, getting water, he started to bathe the blood from her face.

For ten minutes, he worked on her before she recovered; and another fifteen were to pass before she could get her pain-drugged brain to work. She looked through her swollen, discoloured eyelids at the handsome young Texan, and asked weakly: "What happened to me?"

"Just lay back and don't worry about it," Mark replied.

"She beat me!" Pauline gasped. "She *beat* me!"

"Sure. But it's all done now. Lay back and I'll do what I can for you."

"Leave me alone!" there was a note of hysteria in Pauline's voice now. "Just leave me alone."

Mark watched as she rolled over, to hide her face in the pillows. Then he went from the room. For some moments, Pauline lay sobbing. Then she forced her aching body erect and staggered to the dressing-table mirror.

A tangled, matted mass of black hair, surrounding a face which had two half-closed discoloured, puffed-up eyes, a reddened, swollen nose and puffy, cut lips, looked back at her. She stared at the face; the skin, which was once so soft smooth and white, was now tanned and getting coarse. The neck which once was so shapely was now showing the wrinkles of age. Looking down over her bruised and dirty shoulders at the once round, full breasts—which never needed any support to make them conform to the dictates of fashion—she saw they were now drooping and old; and the once-slender waist was developing a roll of fat, which could not be hid. Never until this day had she seen herself like this, a woman no longer young. Never had she known the bitterness of defeat in anything, nor the humiliation of hearing the people of this town jeering at her and calling her an old woman.

The face mocked Pauline from the mirror. She picked up a hair-brush and smashed it into the glass. Then she staggered back to bed and fell across it, with sobs shaking her.

Mark Counter went back to his room; he found his boots, cleaned and shining, waiting for him, and pulled them on. Then he slung the gunbelt round his waist and fastened the thongs about his legs. His face was hard and cold as he went down the stairs and entered the barroom.

Jere Fryer sat at a table separate from his friends. He looked up at Mark, his face suddenly old and drawn, "How is she?" he asked.

"*Do* you care?" Mark's voice was low and vibrant.

To men who knew him, this was a sign that he was starting a temper that would explode into sudden and violent action.

"I care." There was no doubting Fryer's obvious grief. "I surely care more for her than for anything. But I've done bad by her, Mark. Worse than you can ever guess."

"What do you mean?"

"You know I made that bet with Dud Fellowes. I never thought anyone could beat the Major; that was why I bet. Well, I can't get the money for a couple of days, and Fellowes won't wait. I gave him the only thing I've got."

"What was that? Mark's voice was little more than a whisper now.

"The deeds to the Hotel."

Mark's hand gripped the top of the table until the knuckles showed white. "You lost her hotel? After seeing her beaten out there, you gave this place away. You damned no-good handshaker! It'll just about kill her when she finds out."

"I know, Mark. I know. But I never thought she could lose and——!"

Mark's hands shot out across the top of the table, gripping Fryer's lapels and pulling him back over towards Mark. Fryer gave a startled yell and then Mark hit him, smashing home a blow which flung the man across the room and into the wall.

Fryer's friends came to their feet, but stopped as they read murder in the Texan's blue eyes. He stood there, hands hanging near the butts of his matched guns, tense and ready.

"I'm riled, gents. Real riled. The next man who crosses me's going to get hurt bad."

The men watched Mark turn and walk from the bar and out on to the street. "Wonder where he's going?" one asked.

"I don't know," another replied. "But I surely

wouldn't want to cross him.''

Mark went along the nearly deserted street towards the .45 Saloon. The few people who were about were talking excitedly, discussing the fight, and none took any notice of the tall young Texas man.

The saloon was filling up. At the bar were the workers of the place; dealers, bar-tenders, bouncers and girls. Fellowes grinned a greeting as Mark came through the door.

"Come on up and take something on the house, friend. Nobody pays today. I've just won me a hotel.''

"Pauline Cushman's place?'' Mark asked.

At another time, Fellowes would have recognized the tone and been wary; but, at this moment, he was too full of himself to take notice of anything. "Sure. It's just about time that old hag got her come-uppance. She made me close this place on Sundays, and at midnight on every other night. Well, now I've got *her* hotel.'' He roared with laughter. "I knew old Jere couldn't raise five thousand. So I took a chance and, when she got licked, that was all he could give me.''

"It wasn't his place to give,'' Mark replied. "She bought it—changed it from a bug-infested hole to a decent place. You know that?''

"I knew it. But, under Territorial law, a wife's property diverts to her husband. He's the owner under law, not her.''

"Mister, I'll make you a bank draft for the five thousand. The name's Mark Counter. It'll be good.''

"No go, cowhand. I want that hotel.''

"How about Pauline Cushman?''

Fellowes howled with laughter again, not recognizing the deadly savage tone of the Texan's even drawl. "I'll be real good to her. I'll let her be scrub-woman.''

Mark's hands shot out, bunching Fellowes' lapels up, swinging the man clear from his feet and shaking him. Then, with a heave of the great, wide shoulders, Mark hurled the gambler into the bar. Fellowes yelled in pain and dropped to the floor, holding his ribs. He ducked as Mark picked up a chair and hurled it through the bar-mirror.

"Going to take the bank draft now?"

Fellowes glared up at the giant Texan and screamed: "Get him!"

One of the bouncers lunged forward, hands reaching out. Mark gripped a poker table and hefted it as easily as if it'd been made of paper instead of heavy timber. The table swung up and smashed down on to the bouncer's lowered head, dropping him as if he'd been pole-axed.

The other two bouncers came in fast. Mark backhanded one of them hard enough to send him sprawling into the bar, then ducked, caught the other round the knees, straightened and the man went right over. His head smashed into the floor hard enough to put him out of action for a long time.

Mark crossed the room fast. The crowd scattered in front of him—for all knew that any man who stood in the Texan's way was going to get hurt. He halted by the roulette table—Fellowes' pride and joy since its installation by a company which specialized in deliveries after nightfall and offered certain additional fittings not found on more legitimate layouts.

Gripping the edge of the table, Mark's huge muscles bulged up. A man came forward, smashing a bottle and holding the jagged-edged weapon as he lunged across the table. Then Mark heaved. The roulette table was lifted up and thrown over to knock the bottle-wielder backwards. The wheel came loose from its fitting and fell to the floor. Then the table went flying over with a crash that jarred loose certain well-concealed mechanisms.

The one bouncer who could still make his feet was up, but wished he wasn't; for the big Texan fought like a tiger, and with the strength of ten men. The bouncer was picked up. He yelled as his feet left the floor. Then he was sent sprawling into a bunch of saloon employees who showed signs of aggression. The man landed hard, rolling painfully to his knees.

Across the room, Fellowes sat up and his hand went under his coat towards his gun. Mark's right-hand Colt came out, the seven-and-a-half-inch barrel lining as the hammer eared back. Two blue eyes which glowed murder met Fellowes' scared stare, and a deep drawled voice hissed: "Go on, pull it. Just pull it. I never wanted to kill a man so much before!"

Fellowes licked his lips as he watched the Texan advancing on him. He jerked his hand away from the gun-butt and yelled: "Don't touch me. Don't touch me!"

Mark holstered the gun and dragged Fellowes to his feet. He reached into the man's coat and tore the Merwin & Hulbert revolver from its shoulder clip. A man behind the bar dropped his hand underneath for a shotgun—and caught two and a quarter pounds of Merwin gun, thrown with all the strength of a powerful man. He reeled back with blood gushing from his smashed mouth and crashed into the bar, bringing down a couple of bottles from the shelves above him.

Fellowes croaked as the grip changed to his throat and tightened. He was no weakling; but, against such strength as this, he was helpless. The world was roaring round in front of the gambler's eyes. Then he was smashed into the bar again.

"I want that bill-of-sale and I want the deeds for the hotel," Mark said softly.

The gambler clung to the bar and hung there, trying to recover his breath. He saw Mark pick up a chair and throw it across the room, through one of the windows. Then, as the Texan took up a second chair, he gasped: "All right, all right. Take it. Tell Jere Fryer I'll get him for this."

"Mister, I'm not doing this for Jere Fryer. I'm doing it for a woman who's better than this whole stinking town." Mark looked at the townsmen who were there.

"You're all full of pride, because Pauline Cushman got whipped out there. Just you remember one thing: this town is what it is because of that woman. Before a week's gone by, you're going to wish she'd half-killed Iris Pendleton.''

Taking the thick envelope from Fellowes, Mark examined the contents. Then he reached into the front of his shirt. The gambler shook his head. "I don't want your money. Tell Jere I'll collect in a week."

Mark weighed the heavy envelope, then slapped it hard across the gambler's face. "You'll get paid. *I'll* see to that. But stay clear of Pauline Cushman. She's not done yet." He surveyed the sullen bunch of saloon-workers and the scared, awe-filled faces of the towns-people. "I'm going out of here and none of you'd better do anything hasty."

Turning, Mark walked towards the door, watching the faces of the men ahead. He saw the sudden play of expression and whirled, dropping to the floor with hands fanning down. A bar-tender was lifting a shotgun over the bar, his move fast and showing signs of prac-tice; but the shotgun was never made that could lick a Colt Peacemaker for speed of delivery. The long-bar-relled gun in Mark's right hand gave out a spurt of flame and smoke laid whirling eddies round him. The bartender rocked backwards, a hole in his shoulder and his shotgun falling to the bar-top. No other man made an attempt to touch a weapon. Everyone of them knew that the Texan had called his shot for the shoulder. Such lenient treatment would not be afforded to the next man he drew on.

Mark rose, smoke curling lazily from the barrel of his Colt. He looked at Fellowes with contempt and said: "I should kill you right now. But I'll leave you to dirtier hands than mine."

The batwing door swung closed behind Mark Counter and, for a moment, the saloon was silent. Then the townsmen started to walk out, for the first time realising how actions looked. Fellowes watched them go, then looked around the wreck of his saloon, at the broken windows, the smashed barmirror, the broken bottles and the ruined roulette table. That Texan was going to pay for what he'd done. So were Pauline Cushman and Jere Fryer.

"Take care of the place," he snarled to one of the watching men. "I'm going to try and find Big Blue."

Mark Counter felt the anger ebbing from him as he walked back towards the Casa Grande Hotel. He rubbed his hands where they felt sore from slamming into the hard jaw of the bouncer. All-in-all, it had been very satisfactory; the hotel was still in Pauline's hands. Mark knew that he'd made a dangerous enemy in Fellowes, but it gave him little cause for worry. In his life, he'd made a few enemies before, and they never worried him unduly. One more-or-less wouldn't make any difference.

Strangely, he felt less animosity towards Fellowes than to the people of the town. Those smug self-righteous women who posed as ladies, yet stood by and screamed for Iris Pendleton to smash Pauline into the ground. The women whose jealousy for a better woman turned them into hate-filled harridans. Well, they would soon know just what it meant not to have Pauline Cushman running their town, and their lives, for them. It would not be pleasant.

The bar was deserted, except for Jere Fryer, when Mark returned. The man sat at a table with his head in his hands. It was a strained, white face showing a dull bruise where Mark's fist had landed, that looked up. Fryer was shocked and shaken to his core by the magnitude of what he'd done to his wife. Mark studied the face and read the deep misery in it. The man genuinely loved and cared for his wife; and the bet he had taken was but a simple tribute to her prowess.

"Have you seen her?" Mark asked.

"She's still in her room, sobbing something awful. I

can't go in there and tell her what I've done, Mark. It'd
kill her. I'd rather kill myself.''

Mark took the envelope from inside his shirt front,
holding it out. Fryer stared down at it for a long
moment, as if he couldn't believe his eyes. Then he
looked at the reddened knuckles of Mark's left hand
and finally up at the handsome face.

''Wh—Where did you get that?'' Fryer asked.

''Fellowes. He got to thinking that he'd rather have
the money than your place after all. See you pay him
when he wants the money.''

''Sure. Mark sure. I don't know how I can ever thank
you. The Major'll never need to know about this now.''

''Don't be loco—you know someone will tell her.
They'll tell her the same way they told her about you
and that blonde gal. Just to stir up trouble between
Pauline and you,'' Mark snapped back. ''And, Fryer,
this town's going to see some bad trouble. Every two-bit
trouble-causer Pauline ever made act decent around
here'll be headed back here, looking for evens.''

''To hell with them—and this whole stinking town!''
Fryer replied. ''We're going to sell this place and get
out.''

''Running won't get Pauline's self-respect back,''
Mark put in. ''If she leaves here now she's done for.
This town took away her self-respect, and she's got to
get it back here.''

''The lousy scum! Pauline's tamed this town and
made it fit to live in. Then out there they screamed for
Iris Pendleton to thrash her. There were women in that
crowd who wouldn't even speak to Iris, and they were
hanging round her and trying to lick her feet.''

''Sure; that's the way people are. Pauline Cushman
wasn't one of the ordinary herd. She stood taller than
them. And she did things they might have liked to, but
couldn't. Maybe, she tried to run their lives a mite too
much for them, too. So, when she gets into a fight, or
something, they want to see her beaten. That means

she's the same size as the others." Mark stopped for a moment, then went on: "All her life Pauline's been different from the rest. She was a big name in the theatre, a Union Army spy, and she was the law in this town. She was the best at everything she did. Now she's been beaten and she doesn't know what to do. She needs you, Fryer. For the first time in her life, she needs you. Get up to her room and tell her the full story. Don't lie to her. It'll be best."

Fryer pushed back his chair. His hands were shaking as he put the deeds into his coat-pocket. He turned and walked from the bar-room and up the stairs. Mark watched him go and heard him open the door of his wife's room. The big Texan went out and looked along Casa Grande's main street. A quiet, peaceful town lay there before him. All the same, he knew that the quiet and peacefulness would not last much longer. Casa Grande was going to boom into a real, wild, woolly and uncurried frontier town. Maybe, the good citizens weren't going to like it at all.

For two days after the fight, all was quiet in town. Pauline Cushman was in bed all the first day; and, on the second, came out of her room only to check in the wash brought back by the big German girl. She looked over the half-washed sheets with a dull, uninterested stare. Then, dragging her stiff and aching body to the Hotel washhouse, she set to work to rewash the entire bundle.

The Madame of the local cat-house bawled out one of her girls, doing it with one eye on the rear of the Casa Grande Hotel and the other on a nice safe retreat, if Pauline Cushman came. However, there was no sign of the black-haired woman who'd been so forceful in her previous objections; and, by nightfall, the good ladies of the town were listening to the madame's strident, bawling curses, and blushing. If Pauline Cushman heard, the only sign she gave was to shut the windows of her room and endure the heat of the day, rather than to accept that she was no longer the ruler of Casa Grande.

On the evening of the second day, a cowhand let off a shot or two into the air, preparing to light out of town at a dead run. Then, seeing that there was no one to object, he rode the length of main street, firing his revolver and whooping. In a final burst of bravado, he stopped his horse in front of the Casa Grande Hotel and sent three bullets through the sign. He whooped delightedly when no reprisals were taken on him, whirled his horse and headed out of town.

By the end of the week, Casa Grande, as Mark Counter had predicted, was a wild, wide open town. The saloons—once closed at midnight at the risk of having Pauline Cushman shoot up the fittings if they stayed open longer—stayed open all night. The erstwhile peace of Sunday found the hymn-singing at the church battling for supremacy, and failing to drown out the tinny pianos and screeching violins of the saloons and dance-halls.

Cowhands from the local ranches swaggered the streets in bunches, hoorawing the local citizens. Mule-skinners came in from the railroad construction camps and the burly railroad men arrived to add their wild cursing and hell-raising to the never-closed, always-going sounds of the once peaceful town of Casa Grande.

Through all of this Pauline Cushman stayed in her room as much as possible, appearing only when forced to do so. The marks of the fight left her face, but there were other, deeper scars that did not heal. She heard, second-hand, that the ladies of the town—in a desperate attempt to prove that their town was still the same quiet and peaceable place it had been under Pauline Cushman's strong rule—were going to organise a dance. This was a direct snub for her, and she knew it. In the past, she not only organised the dances, but attended to every detail of them with her usual care and attention; she selected the band, arranged for the callers, fixed up the food and selected the dances which were to be played. This time, the town aimed to show that they could do without Pauline Cushman; and the more catty members wanted to ask Iris Pendleton to run the affair.

This latter was objected to by the more sedate and wiser heads—for her rise to fame appeared to have gone to Iris' blonde head. Her hotel, a small, not-too-clean place, was filled with travelling men, who would otherwise have stayed at the Casa Grande. She was thinking of arranging to have her portrait painted, standing victorious over Pauline Cushman. This would look good behind the bar in her place, and would give added colour to the forlorn looking bundle of black hair hanging there now.

Yet more than just her fortune changed with the fight. She took on a fresh glow and bought a Colt revolver and gunbelt, wearing them openly and amusing the guests at her hotel by what she fondly imagined was a fast draw. Her manner grew imperious; and she attended a meeting of the ladies sewing circle, there to give unwanted advice to the other ladies.

Mark Counter watched all this as he sat on the porch of the Casa Grande Hotel and whittled a stick. The crowd passed him by, and none of the whooping, hard-drinking men interfered with him. Only once was it tried. A mule-skinner went along to the Casa Grande Hotel to tree Pauline Cushman on her own ground. What Mark did to that man warned off every other. The man was a week before he could walk. When he could, he left town as fast as a good horse could carry him.

The blood-bay was well enough to travel by then, but Mark stayed on—not meaning to leave until Pauline was back to something like her old self again. All too well, he knew that she could never be the old Pauline Cushman; but she could be better than that hollow shell of a woman hiding away in her room.

It was a fortnight after the fight and the morning of

the dance. Mark Counter walked towards the local store, noting the glances the mothers of grown-up and unmarried daughters gave him. Since word had gone out as to who he was, and that he was the son of one of the richest men in Texas, he had been given plenty of attention.

The owner of the store—a fat, cheerful-looking man of Germanic origin, who was called Dutchy by most people in town—looked up. He was serving a couple of women; Mark was quite willing to wait—he wanted to buy a couple of new pairs of socks, and was in no hurry.

Iris Pendleton came in, the heavy Colt bouncing against her leg as she crossed the room and slapped on the countertop. "Come on here, Dutchy. I'm in a hurry," she called. "The girls don't mind waiting. Do you girls?"

The two women looked up angrily, but neither objected. With a sigh of resignation, the store-keeper turned to Iris. However, she'd seen Mark, and ignored the waiting shopkeeper.

"Mark," she said, smiling condescendingly at him. "Didn't you get my message to come and stay down at my place?"

"Sure, I got it."

"When will you be coming then?" she asked.

"I won't. I like the Casa Grande Hotel."

"And old Pauline Cushman?" Iris purred, moving nearer to the tall Texan. "I hear you've been seeing a lot of her—and looking after her interests far better than her husband can."

Mark's eyes narrowed; he hated to see a nice, friendly young woman like Iris Pendleton so puffed up with conceit that she was spoiling herself. He also did not like her attitude, nor her insinuations.

"I don't see any more of Pauline than you used to of her husband."

Her eyes snapped angrily at him. "Did Pauline Cushman say that about me?"

"No. *I* did. I'll tell you something; you're so puffed up with conceit because you licked a woman maybe twenty years older than yourself. Why ten years, or even five, back, she'd have chased you clear out of this town—you and two like you."

"How dare you speak to me like that!" Iris hissed, her eyes blazing in fury.

"Why'd you fight Pauline in the first place?" Mark asked.

"She called me a whore."

"Then don't act like one."

Iris screamed and swung a slap at Mark's face. Steel-hard fingers caught her wrist before the hand touched flesh. Mark contemptuously shoved her hand away from him and she fell back against the counter. Her hand dropped, fumbling the Colt clear and lifting it.

Mark moved forward, his hand slapping the gun down, landing on the firm white flesh of her wrist hard enough to make her let the weapon fall. Then he gripped the wrist, sat down and spun her across his knee. His hand rose and fell hard across the tight expanse of frock which covered her rump. Iris struggled, screamed and used some language a polite young lady should not have known existed. However, as the hard hand rose and fell, the angry yells turned to painfilled sobs and she kicked helplessly over his knee.

At last, Mark stood the sobbing girl up and shook her, forcing her tear-stained face to look up at his. "Don't you ever, as long as you live, pull a gun on a man again!" he snapped. "Now, get in the line there, if you want serving. You're trying to make like you're another Pauline Cushman. Well, you aren't, and never can be. Go on, get out of here and try to stop being something you can't. Folks like you for what you are. They laugh at you when you try to be Pauline Cushman."

Iris turned and half-ran from the store, tears falling down her cheeks more from humiliation than from

pain. She heard the laughter of the other women of the
town, and knew the story would be all round soon.
She'd thought they regarded her as they had Pauline
Cushman. Now she knew different. Even the men at her
hotel thought of her gun-toting as a joke.

Dutchy Klein sighed as he watched Iris leave the store.
He finished serving, then came to Mark, who lounged
against the counter.

"It's a great pity, Mark. She was a nice young woman
before the fight. Sure she was a bit loud. But she'd
been widowed and, before that, worked in a dance-
hall. I reckon she'd soon have been accepted by the
women-folk if she hadn't licked Pauline Cushman. She
changed from that day. It made her swelled-headed: she
wouldn't wait to be served, always pushed in front. Is a
great pity. I'm sorry for her."

"And me. Maybe she'll change now."

"I hope so. What can I get for you?"

The dance was not a success. First, the band was not
present; and, too late, the committee who were running
things realised that no one had told any of the musicians
what time they were to arrive, or what to play. Then two
of the ladies discovered that neither had ordered the
buffet from the Eating House, and there was a mad rush
to prepare things. Then, when the guests arrived, the
women found still more worry and trouble for themselves. With Pauline Cushman running the dance the
local cowhands were always on their best behaviour.
With her not even present, they came wild and rowdy.

The first few dances showed the trend; there was wild
swinging of partners and horse-play on the floor. Then
the band stopped playing in mid-tune, the music dying
off as the five pieces of the orchestra saw the men who
stood in the doorway.

Big Blue grinned around at the startled and worried
faces. His long blacksnake whip exploded in a roaring
crack.

"I'm a ring-tailed ripper and it's my time to howl!" he screamed. "Anybody who wants good fun, come and follow me."

The cowhands—who were no lovers of mule-skinners at other times—whooped their approval. This was better than any old dance with a load of lemon-sour-faced women watching your every move. They howled their delight and streamed from the room, following Big Blue and the mule-skinners.

From across the street, Fellowes watched the men streaming out of the church and grinned. Pauline Cushman was going to wish she'd never been borne when Big Bill and his men got through with her. The gambler returned to his saloon and waited until the men came streaming in. Then he roared: "Drink on the house, boys."

Fellowes got his first inclination that not only Pauline Cushman would suffer when one of his bar-dogs tried to take pay for the second lot of drinks. The mule-skinner roared in rage and dragged the bar-tender over the counter. Another of the mule-skinners leapt over and started to pour out liquor, freely and wildly. When one of the bouncers tried to stop this, the crowd went wild. The fight roared through Fellowes's .45 Saloon, wrecking it and leaving not as much as one unbroken chair.

Then the drunken mob—for they helped themselves to all they wanted—left and outside looked round. For all he was drunk, Big Blue remembered those cold, contemptuous black eyes facing him and realised that he was not yet ready to face Pauline Cushman. So, at the head of his bunch, he tramped into the next saloon —where the owner, having heard of, and given his unspoken blessing to Fellowes's plan, welcomed them.

Never was a town to get such a treeing. It made the efforts of Clay Allison on a rampage look mild and gentle. The crowd went the length of Main Street and hardly left a whole window, yet they steered clear of the

Casa Grande Hotel. Big Blue was saving that for his last effort—when he'd worked his mob, and himself, up to the right pitch. So they went on round the town, a wild shouting, reckless mob.

Mark Counter lay on his bed and listened to the noise. He had stayed away from the dance and, after a time, rose to go out along the passage to the head of the staircase. Several townspeople came crowding and more followed. Along the street flames licked up from a building.

"They're firing Fellowes's saloon!" a man yelled.

More men and women crowded in; the German washerwoman, the madame from the brothel and Iris Pendleton were among the last to arrive. All showed fear and anxiety as they entered.

"Mr. Counter," the storekeeper called, as he saw the Texan at the head of the stairs. "Would you please come down here."

Mark walked down the stairs, looking round at the crowd and reading the fear in every face. He stepped down to walk across the room, every eye on him.

"Mr. Counter, we all know you and your reputation. We want you to be our town marshal."

"Thank you very much," Mark replied. He looked round the room. They were all here, the women and the men who had jeered Pauline Cushman as she lay beaten on the ground. "You want me to go out there and face down that mob. That's what you mean."

"You could do it," a woman spoke up.

"I *might* be able to—but I don't aim to. There is only one way a man could stop that mob out there, and that is to kill some of them. That I don't aim to do."

"We'd pay you well," a man put in. "They're running wild out there. All the way along Main Street, there isn't a whole window. The town will be a wreck——"

"And *why!*" Mark ignored the imputation that he sold his guns. "I'll tell you why. Because a woman was beaten in that corral out there. Not beaten by another woman, but by something she couldn't lick—time. Pauline Cushman held this town under and made it fit for you to live in. Then, when she got beaten, you didn't show her any feeling. You yelled for Iris Pendleton there, like she'd done something great. You left Pauline Cushman lying out there like she was the leader of a herd of buffalo after he's been whipped by a younger bull. Now you're seeing what it means. Pauline Cushman is the only one in the world who might have held this thing in check, and I wouldn't blame her if she told you to go to hell. Just like I'm doing."

Jere Fryer turned on his heel: he was standing at the end of the room and looking down the street. "They're gathering. Big Blue's talking to them, and he's pointing down here."

The crowd moved closer together, as if trying to gain more security from the proximity with the others. At the back, Iris Pendleton looked at the German washerwoman, then at the owner of the brothel. She started to speak, but the words choked in her throat. The madame fluffed up her feather boa and nodded. Without needing any telling what the others planned, all three went up the stairs.

Jere Fryer looked round the room. He went to the bar and took out a box from underneath, removing a Smith & Wesson revolver from it. He broke the gun open and checked on the loads, then looked round.

"Who'll come with me?" he asked.

Not one man in the crowd moved, even his cronies standing fast and immobile. One man spoke up, his voice sullen. "You can't expect us to go out there and fight them, Jere. We're not fighting men."

"Neither am I." Fryer looked round at the faces in front of him. "Mark called me a hand-shaker and that about covers me. I was just a shadow living on Pauline Cushman's reputation. It's time I tried to live on my own."

One of the men who'd been on the balcony stepped

from the crowd, went to the bar and took the second
Smith & Wesson from the box. "Never want it said
Mike Rice won't back his friend," he said and walked
forward.

The two men walked towards the door. They were
almost at it—and, outside, the rumble and yells of the
mob grew louder and louder as Big Blue worked his
courage up to make the big plunge that would see if
Pauline Cushman really had lost her nerve.

Mark Counter rose from the chair he'd taken,
loosened the matched guns and went forward. He
grinned at Fryer, then looked back at the crowd. "I
wouldn't lift a hand for the rest of this town. But I'll go
with you right now."

They stepped to the door. Mark looked out to where,
in the light of the burning saloon, Big Blue and his men
stood in half-decision. Mark glanced at the other two;
they were pale but their faces showed determination.
However, he thought he'd better give them some advice:

"When we get out there, you go to the right side of
the trail, Mike. You take the left, Jere. I'll stop in the
centre. If it comes to talking, let me do it. But, if it
comes to shooting, hit the ground and fight from there.
Shoot as fast as you can and hug the sidewalk."

The men fanned out as they stepped from the hotel;
Mike Rice crossing the street, Mark taking the centre
and Jere Fryer standing at the left. They stood still for a
moment, then started to move forward.

Big Blue saw the men coming towards him. He
noted the way the big Texan moved, the way his hands
brushed the butts of those guns; and he knew that,
whatever was to happen, here was a man who would not
back water. Here was the real thing, a two-gun fighting
man who knew his business from soda to hock, and was
willing to back his play with smoking guns.

The other men in the crowd knew, too; they were not
so drunk that they did not know that they'd carried
things as far as possible without shooting. All stood

waiting to hear what their self-appointed leader, Big Blue, decided. The mule-skinner licked his lips, watching the handsome blond giant halt, hands hanging with fingers slightly flexed and legs braced apart. It was the stance of a skilled gun-fighter and one ready to practise his art.

"What you want?" the mule-skinner asked.

"Nothing. Just standing here and making sure that you boys don't come any nearer," Mark Counter replied.

"Is that so?" Big Blue snarled. "Did you hear that, boys?"

There was an ugly rumble through the crowd and the men started to fan out, ready to advance.

Pauline Cushman lay on her bed, staring dully at the roof. She saw the leaping light of the flames rolling skywards and heard the howl of the drunken mob. It stirred her no more than the sound of breaking windows, or the fighting. She was too uninterested to care what the men out there did—even if, as she suspected, her own place was to be next.

There was a knock on the door, and it opened. She came off her bed as the three women came in. She looked at each one—the madame, the washerwoman and Iris Pendleton.

"Pauline, you've got to stop them!" Iris Pendleton was finding what Pauline Cushman knew. That crow is an evil tasting bird to eat. "Only you can."

"They haff tore down all mine vashings and dragged them in the dirt," the big German woman went on. "And, when I tried to stop them, they threatened to burn my home."

"They been through my house and took all the gals they wanted. Not one of 'em would pay a dime. Just about wrecked my place," the madame put in. "And they just about wrecked the rest of the town. Your place is next."

"They nearly wrecked mine." There was grief and pain in Iris Pendleton's tones: "Look, Pauline, that husband of yours, he never came near me——"

Pauline Cushman rolled from the bed and stood up; for a moment there was some of the old fire in her eyes. "Don't lie, Mrs. Pendleton. I know Jere Fryer. He could no more resist hanging round you than a dog round an on-heat bitch. I don't think much of his taste, nor of yours."

Iris hung her head; the pride she'd felt at beating this almost legendary woman was bitter as gall now. She knew that, although she had smashed Pauline Cushman down in physical combat, she would never be the better woman.

"A man told me that ten years ago, or even five, you'd have beaten me," she said. "It's true. I even tried to act like you after our fight. But there is only one Pauline Cushman."

"Your husband's going out there to face that crowd. Him, that Mark Counter and young Mike Rice," the madame said from the window.

Pauline pushed by the other woman and looked down into the street. All too well she knew that Jere Fryer was no fighting man, and only a very average performer with a gun. She also knew that no three men could halt that crowd, without shooting and killings.

"Get my rifle from that cupboard!" it was the Major, Pauline Cushman, the Scout of the Cumberland, talking again. "Move, one of you! Hand me my shoes, Mrs. Soehnen."

The other three stood by in silent admiration as the Major pulled on her shoes, then checked the loads in her rifle and strode out of the door. The madame turned and looked Iris up and down. "I hear you've got some of her hair hung over your bar. Take it down and burn it—or, by all that's holy, I'll come down there and do it myself."

"And, if she can't, I help her," the washerwoman

finished. "You help me collect all the washing. It ain't been done so good these last few days."

Big Blue and his crowd started their advance down the street. Mark Counter stood fast, ready to make his move when it became necessary. He watched the other men coming closer. "That's far enough!"

Mark's words cut like a knife across at the others. Big Blue knew that he'd pushed this as far as he could, without shooting. Then he considered the facts. At his back was a large bunch of men; facing him were two men who weren't good with guns and one who was probably very good. The odds would never be better in his favour than they were at that moment.

"Come on, boys!" he yelled.

"Blue! You dirty mule-ruining, no good rat!"

Big Blue stopped in his tracks. From the side of a building. into the light of the fire, stepped Pauline Cushman, her Winchester lined full on him. He took an involuntary pace backwards towards the crowd.

"I heerd you wus done," he mumbled.

"You did, did you?" The beautiful black eyes lashed the crowd with scorn. "I know every man of you here. Get off into the brush and sleep this off. Then, tomorrow, I want you all back to clean up the mess you've made in town. Understand?"

The men in the crowd stood immobile. Then, slowly, they started to break up and a drunken cowhand whooped: "Good for you, Major!"

A figure lurched from the side of the street, a wild-eyed man in the torn and dishevelled remains of a gambler's fancy rig. He halted and from under his coat, he brought out a short-barrelled Marwin & Hulbert revolver, to line in on Pauline Cushman.

"You old witch!" Fellowes gasped. "I've lost my saloon, and your place is still standing. I'm going to kill you."

Jere Fryer forgot his gun, he hurled forward in be-

tween his wife and Fellowes just as the gambler triggered off a shot. Fryer crashed back into his wife, blood
oozing from his shoulder. At the same instant, Mark
Counter's right-hand gun came out with a flickering
blur of speed. The hammer eased back under his thumb
even as the gun was lifting and, by the time it lined,
all was set. The hammer fell and flame tore from the
muzzle. Fellowes rocked backwards as lead took him.
Even as he went down, he triggered off one more shot.
Then the gun slid from his hand. He arched his back,
then went limp.

Mark stepped forward and looked down. One glance
told him that it was all over, and that Dudley Fellowes
had fallen to his hand.

Pauline Cushman was holding her husband. She
glared at the crowd. "Big Blue, give Mark a hand here.
Get Jere back to the hotel."

"Yes'm. I'll do just that," Big Blue replied.

Mike Rice joined Mark Counter and wiped sweat
from his face. The crowd was disbanding now. The
young townsman watched Pauline Cushman standing in
the centre of the street, directing the men to return the
following morning—or she'd want to know why.

"That's the Major," Rice remarked. "She sure is
some woman."

Mark grinned back. "She surely is."

Mark Counter saddled his big stallion, ready to leave
Casa Grande the morning after the hoorawing. From
the places where they'd been sage-henning, the cowhands and mule-skinners had returned. They were being
put to work on clearing up the wreckage by Pauline
Cushman.

"Mr. Counter, sir." It was the photographer standing there, holding out a developed picture and an exposed plate. "I took this of the Major after the fight. I
burnt all the pictures I'd developed, but this one.
Now." He took out a match, lit it and burned the piece
of paper, then dropped the plate and, lifting his foot,

stamped it to pieces. "I wouldn't make money on a thing like that."

Mark gripped his hand, then turned to find Pauline Cushman bearing down on him. The photographer turned and hurried away and Pauline smiled up at the big Texan. "I hope you enjoyed your stay in Casa Grande."

"Sure, I'll never forget it. One thing though, Major: you're retired from the Army now; try and remember it."

"Meaning?"

"Let other folks make some of the decisions some of the time. That way, they could get to like you, instead of just respecting you."

She threw back her head and laughed. "I'll remember that. I've promised to lend Iris Pendleton a hand with her place, to get it going again. Funny, when I went to see her, she was burning some hair."

Mark laughed. He looked at the woman they called the Major, swept off his hat in a graceful bow and kissed her hand. Swinging into the saddle of the blood-bay he looked down at her.

"You know something, Major. If you'd ever met Belle Boyd, I'd bet you'd have held her to the tightest-drawn fight ever seen."

Pauline laughed back. "You damned Reb," she replied. "Call in again some time and see us all. I'd best go and nurse my invalid now."

Mark Counter rode slowly from the town of Casa Grande and, from the top of a rim, turned and looked back. His visit had cost him thirty dollars, and the bet; but it was worth it and more—for he'd helped restore a good woman's self-respect.

CHAPTER FIVE

Stomp Hollorhan's Boast

Red Blaze never expected to win the bet. He explained that to the others of the floating outfit as they sat round the table in the gun-decorated room Ole Devil Hardin used as a study.

"Fact being," he'd remarked to his wholly unsympathetic audience. "You bunch should ought to give me odds of five-to-one at least."

Not that Red was a trouble-causer, or even a trouble-hunting man. It was just that, as some people have a way of finding gold, or fish in a river, Red Blaze found trouble.

It came as something of a shock to him to be riding into Pinto City, the second town on his itinerary, without having to fight someone for making fun of his hair colour.

Red Blaze had hair that was untidy, long and red. His expensive brown JB Stetson hat was shoved back to show the frontal mass of his hair and expose his pugnaciously good-looking and freckled face to the sun. Around his throat, tight-rolled and knotted, was a silk bandana which contained near on every colour imaginable in a gorgeous riot which defied description. Red was proud of the bandana, more so than of any other thing he owned. Ole Devil had given it to him to show approval of Cousin Red's first lone-hand chore and of how he'd handled it.

The bandana hung long ends over his dark red shirt, almost to the waistband of his brown levis. The cuffs of the levis were turned back and hung outside his expensive and fancy-stitched boots. Around his waist was a buscadero gun-belt, walnut-butted Colt Cavalry Peacemakers butt-forward in the holsters.

He rode his big clayback stallion easily, the good Texas kak saddle between his knees. He had his rope strapped to the horn, bed-roll to the cantle; and, from under his left leg, there showed the butt of his Spencer carbine.

Red studied the town of Pinto with the gaze of a man who'd looked on such capitals of the cow-country as Dodge City, Wichita, Hays, Abilene and Fort Worth. His reason for coming here was to deliver an invitation to the lawman, Stomp Hollorhan. Ole Devil had checked Red's route and asked him to call in to ask Hollorhan to make a visit to the Rio Hondo when he retired.

So Red Blaze was surveying the town of Pinto and thinking how little it differed from any of the many sun and heat-dried towns throughout the range country. It consisted in the main of one long street—which provided a man with the chance and facilities to be born at the doctor's, attend school, get married buy and furnish a house with everything it might ever need, get drunk, gamble, be put in jail, post mail, have his horse shoed or stabled; and, at the end of his days, wind up on a slab in the sombre parlour of the undertaker's shop.

In fact, there was not a single dwelling on main street that was not a business of some kind. Only two places of community value which were not on Main Street were the opposites and at opposing sides of the town. They were the church and the brothel. The church was situated on the better side of town, along with the homes, in order of prosperity, of the two saloon-keepers, the undertaker, the better-off business men and the town-dwellings of the big ranch owners. At the other side lived the town marshal and the rest of the citizens.

Taken all in all, Pinto was hardly the sort of town where a man would expect to find old Stomp Hollorhan. In his day he'd made a name as a lawman which left tarnished the better-publicised efforts of such practitioners of the silver star as Dallas Stoudenmire, Longhair Jim Courtney, or Bat Masterson. He'd tamed the bad wild towns just after the War—when a Southern lawman was harder to find than a snowball in hell. Now he was here in a small, one-horse town like Pinto; and, soon, if the word was right, he would be retiring.

Along the street a piece, where it widened out to allow stage coaches turning room and to make a town square, a crowd was gathered round a garishly-coloured wagon. From his seat on the big claybank thoroughbred, Red looked over the scene and a grin which was never long absent from his face broadened. He'd seen many Medicine Shows in his time, but never missed one if he could help it.

"Doctor Henry Folsom's Miracle Balsam and Tonic."

The words were emblazoned on the side of the wagon in large and eye-catching letters. Red rode slowly round to get a view of the rear, which was painted to represent a trail-end town. The back of the wagon was let down and formed a stage on which a pretty, blonde woman, wearing a green satin dress, was playing a guitar and singing *Barbara Allen*.

Like most folks in the West, Red enjoyed a medicine show. The travelling mendicants brought a chance for the womenfolk, especially the poorer ones, to see a show. In Texas, particularly in the smaller towns of the time, there were few theatres; and a good woman did not go into a saloon where the only other professional entertainers appeared. So, even if the magical medicines did fall short of their maker's claims, the shows themselves were well-received.

The girl stopped her song with a flourish and acknowledged the cheers of the crowd. Then she announced: "And now we present for your entertainment, *The Man Of A Thousand Faces.*"

A tall, slim, young man with a thin, aristocratic face stepped out. He wore a collarless shirt, trousers and moccasins. "Ladies and gentlemen," he said. "I would like to introduce you to a few people you may know."

He stepped back into the wagon and, in a couple of seconds, a different man emerged. Now long hair flowed to his shoulders and a vast handlebar moustache was under a nose which was as hooked as the beak of a bald eagle. He wore a fancy buckskin outfit and, sticking out from various parts of his body, as if they were buried into him, were the hilts of several knives. In his belt were four revolvers, two bowie knives, a tomahawk and a bundle of scalps.

The crowd burst into roars of laughter for all had seen caricatures of Wild Bill Hickok in different newspapers. The girl stepped forward and looked up at this larger-than-life imitation of Hickok.

"Why Wild Bill," she greeted. "Where have you been?"

"Fighting the McCanles gang. 'Twarn't much of a fight though—only fifteen of them."

Probably, only Red in the crowd realised how good the impersonation was, even to Wild Bill's booming, boastful voice.

"But your wounds—don't they hurt?"

"Only when I laugh!"

Wild Bill disappeared to roars of Texas laughter—for the true story of Hickok's "Great Fight" with the terrible McCanles gang was well known in Texas. It was also known that the stories of the fight now circulating were far less truthful, but far more creditable to Wild Bill.

Another man came from the back of the wagon and Red stared in amazement, thinking for a moment it was Wyatt Earp who stood there. It was amazing; the sober black coat, hat and trousers; the look of sanctimonious piety; the drooping moustache—they were all as Red remembered seeing on his visit to Dodge. The man came forward, the barrel of his revolver so long that it almost dragged on the floor.

Again, a roar of laughter greeted the appearance—for everyone there had also seen the cartoons of Wyatt Earp.

"Mr. Earp," the girl said, to make sure everyone knew who this was. "Why are you like a Scottish horse-shoer?"

"I don't know, Miss Bella. Why am I like a Scottish horse-shoer?" Again, the voice was completely right.

"Because you're a Mac—and you're black-smithing."

The crowd roared at this—even the ladies, who were not supposed to know that a "Mac" was a pimp who worked at procuring for the red light trade and "blacksmithing" meant living on the immoral earnings of the prostitutes. This was a typical joke in Texas—for Wyatt Earp, and the rest of the Kansas law-and-order crowd, were suspected by the Texans of, if not actually owning and operating, at least, getting their fair share of the profits of the red light area.

Red swung down from his claybank and fastened it to the rail; he lounged on the sidewalk, ready to enjoy the rest of the show. Then, from out of town, there came an interruption in the shape of eight hard-riding, wild-shooting, loud-yelling Texas cowboys. This did not un-duly worry Red; he'd come to town that way himself before now—except that the floating outfit made sure their wild riding did not endanger anyone. This bunch were not so particular as they came barrelling into the crowd, scattering the people all ways.

The dust died down and the young cowhands sat their horses, looking in delighted fashion at the scattered citizens. Two of them caught Red's eye right away as the leaders of the bunch. One was a tall, handsome you man dressed better than the other hands and riding a thoroughbred. Around his waist was an expensive hand-tooled gunbelt with an ivory-handled Colt Artillery Peacemaker in the holster. It was the rig of a fast man with a gun, yet—unless Red was far wrong in his guess—this young man was no gunfighter. His face was tanned, good-looking and showed some breeding.

The other was different; from his hat to his boots he spelled trouble. Red could read the signs and knew that here was the kind of yahoo who got all cowhands a bad name. There was a sullen truculence about him that could mean he was very good with a gun or thought he was.

The slender man stepped from the back of his wagon again and looked down at the eight cowhands, then at his erstwhile audience, who were headed for home and safety.

"Howdy, boys. Now you've had your fun, how about staying to see the show?"

The truculent hand grinned. He shook loose his rope and flipped it over one of the wagon wheels. "See the show?" he mimicked. "We *are* the show!"

Saying this, he dallied his rope and sent the horse leaping forward. The rope twanged tight and ripped the wheel clean from the wagon. Folsom yelled as his wagon tipped over. He caught the girl and leapt clear with her, as, from inside, sounded the crash of breaking bottles.

"Brock!" the handsome youngster snapped, angrily. "There wasn't any need for that."

"Jest funning around, Tad, just funning," the other replied, grinning at the others. "Come on down to the saloon."

A tall oldster came from the sidewalk and stepped through the circle of wide-grinning cowhands. He glared from under fierce, bushy eyebrows, his lined, seamed old face showing anger. He glared up at the young man called Tad and snapped: "I warned ye, last time you was in town, Tad Cooke. Now I'm jailing you."

"We were only funning, Stomp," Cooke replied. "I'll pay for the damage."

Stomp Hollorhan shook his head grimly. "A spell in pokey is all you'll understand, so I'm taking——"

The man called Brock jumped his horse forward, his Colt coming out and slamming down on to the old lawman's head, dropping him to the ground.

"Eeyah!" Brock screamed delightedly. "Come on, boys. Down to the saloon and get us likkered up."

Tad Cooke watched the others going, then followed them. Doc Folsom swore under his breath; he clenched his hands, looking towards the wagon. The girl caught his arm, whispering: "No Frank. Not this time, please."

So Folsom went and bent over the old-timer, turning him gently on to his back. He looked down at the black-and-white calfskin vest and white shirt which was Stomp Hollorhan's trade-mark, then at the tarnished badge which had seen use in many a wild town. A hand came over his shoulder, then an arm with a dark red sleeve. The badge was unpinned and lifted back.

Folsom straightened and looked round. He found a tall, red-haired young man pinning the badge on his shirt. Then loosening the guns in their holsters, the young man walked down the street.

The cowhands were in a group outside one of the saloons. Tad Cooke glared at Brock and snapped, "You're going too far. There was no need for what you did to old Stomp."

"Now, Tad boy. You're just thinking about his granddaughter, not him. Anyhow, that ringy old goat shouldn't come interfering with us."

"All right, all of you, turn round."

The cowhands turned to find Red Blaze bearing down on them. He halted facing them and looked them over while they studied him and the badge he was wearing.

"What do you want?" Brock asked.

"I'm taking you in." The voice was flat and even.

"Look here, friend." Tad Cooke stepped forward, holding out his hand. "I'm real sorry for what happened to old Stomp. Brock shouldn't have done it. But we've been out on the range for a month and this is our first time in town. We'll pay for any damage we've done and hold it down some."

"Mister, there are a dozen things I'm taking you for: Assault on a law officer; reckless riding; discharging firearms in the city limits. Destruction of——"

"Just hark at him, boys," Brock whooped. "Ain't he the living wonder, the way he spouts it all?"

The cowhands closed around Red and one of them leaned forward, pressing hard against his left side. Then Brock's hand went down towards his gun. In his eyes was the light of killing lust, for he was thinking of the cross-draw and, with a man pinning the left gun and arm, Brock had the red-head whipsawed.

Red Blaze might be a hot-headed young man who acted without thinking and was apt to jump into any fight without worrying about consequences; but, once in, he was cool and capable. His right hand twisted back around the walnut grip of the right-side gun and brought it out in a smoothly-done cavalry twist. The gun was out and lined an instant before Brock's. Flame tore from the muzzle of the Colt and Brock rocked back on his heels. Red hated to be forced into killing, but he knew that the young man would kill him, given the chance.

Even as lead drove into Brock, Red Blaze slammed his elbow into the stomach of the man at his left, doubling him over. Then, savagely, he smashed the long barrel of the Colt on to the hand's head.

"Freeze, all of you!" Red snapped, throwing the gun forward, full-cocked and ready. "There's been enough killing already."

The cowhands stood fast; their month-long range work had given them the desire to have fun but this was no longer funny. Yet they admitted that Brock and his bunkie had brought this on themselves. That was not fun they'd just tried, but a deliberate attempt at murder.

"Pick him up and head for the jail," Red snapped. "I'll get this one taken to the undertakers."

The cowhands went ahead, carrying their limp and unconscious pard with them. Red stayed behind only long enough to tell two of the men to take Brock to his last restingplace. Then he followed the others to the jail.

A pretty, tall and shapely girl with hair as red as Red Blaze's untidy thatch was in the office. She stared as the cowhands came in and laid their burden down on the floor. Then her eyes went to Tad Cooke and she asked: "What was that shot? And where's Brock?"

"Dead. Red here killed him. It was a fair fight—though I don't think that will bother Brock's brother."

The girl looked at Red Blaze, then at the star on his shirt. She knew that star well enough; and it was her one ambition in life to get hold of it and give it a good shining. However, it should not be on the shirt of a tall, red-haired young man, no matter how efficient he looked.

"Where's Gramps?" she snapped angrily. "And what are you doing here?"

"Stomp'll be all right, Tildy Mae," Red replied. "Just have him a sore head for a spell—then he'll be mean and ornery as ever. Open up the cells. I'm tossing this bunch in. I'll fill in the charge-book."

"Sore head?" She sounded grim.

"Brock pistol-whipped him," Tad Cooke spoke up, never taking his eyes from the girl. "I'm sorry, but he did it before I could guess what he meant to do."

"I told you that loud-mouthed no-good would end you in trouble, Tad Cooke. But you wouldn't listen to me. All right, I want fifty dollars as surety for the good behaviour of your bunch—and another fifty for fines for whatever Red there charges you with. Put up, or go in.''

The cowhands went into a huddle and then, grumbling, dug out their money. After the fine, there wouldn't be much left for a wild time in town; but they knew better than to argue with Tildy Mae Hollorhan—for the girl had a temper as quick as her grandfather, and she was liable to lock them up for a spell if the money was not forthcoming.

''Tad,'' she snapped, as the cowhands trooped towards the door, ''keep away from the bank. Don't draw any more money out.''

Tad Cooke's face flushed angrily. He turned and slammed the door. Red went and opened it again. ''Hey, you left one,'' he called.

The cowhands carried their pard out; he was groaning his way to consciousness again. They were passed at the door by Folsom and the girl helping Stomp Hollorhan in. Tad Cooke stopped in front of the slim man and said: ''I'm real sorry about what Brock did, mister. Tell me how much damage was done, and I'll make you out a money order against the bank here.''

''Thanks for the offer,'' Folsom replied. ''I'll let you know.''

''Where they at?'' Stomp Hollorhan growled as he was pushed firmly, but gently into a chair by his granddaughter. ''Damn it to hell, Tildy Mae, some damned no-good, no-account ornery thief done wide-looped my badge.''

''Here it is, Stomp. I kinda borrowed it for a spell,'' Red replied. ''Be real obliged to wear it for you until you're well again.''

''Would, would ye!'' Stomp scowled up at Red, suspiciously. ''I suppose Tildy Mae's fetched ye in, though I don't know who ye be.''

''Name's Red Blaze, Ole Devil's nephew.''

''Ole Devil Hardin's kin!'' Stomp snorted. ''I suppose that ole goat allows I'm past culling out the bad ones in this town, does he?''

"Nope, just sent me to ask you to come over for a spell. Got some corn-likker in from Kentucky, and wants your opinion of it—when you've retired, that is.''

"Well, I ain't retired yet. And I won't while there's a bad bunch in this town. So you can head right back and tell him that.''

Tildy Mae moved in between her grandfather and Red, ignoring the young man and using her own kind of tact to get the old man out of the room. She returned and looked at Folsom, then at the young woman and lastly at Red.

"I think all of you'd better get out of town. Jack Brocksen will hear about his brother and come here after you. He'll blame every one of you for Brock getting shot.''

"Never was a hand at running, except from angry redheads who didn't have sense enough to stay off ole Jimmo's mule,'' Red replied.

"I haven't forgotten that, Red Blaze,'' Tildy Mae answered. She came round the desk and kicked him hard across the ankle. Tell your cousin Dusty he'll get the same when I meet him.''

Red yelled and hopped on one leg while he rubbed the other. "You've done it now. I can't walk out of here all crippled up.''

"I'm afraid we're stuck here until we make enough money to move on, too,'' Folsom put in mildly.

Tildy Mae looked at the other woman; there was no animosity in her gaze, for she regarded, despite Eastern ideas, all women as equals. Bella Folsom was a star in her own right to Tildy Mae's way of thinking; and at least a social equal to any saloon-keeper's wife.

"Can't you talk sense into them?'' she asked.

"Not Frank, when he gets in this sort of mood. Besides, we could use the money.''

"Look, Red. Do you know what sort of town this is?"

"Just a cattle-town to me," Red replied.

"Sure, just a one-horse cattle-town. Not much for a man who ran the law in Fort Worth, San Antone, or Austin in the wild days. But it's Stomp Hollorhan's town. Even if it is the last one. And you know Stomp Hollorhan's boast?"

"About never leaving a wild bunch in a town for the next man. Sure I've heard of it. He kept the Governor of Texas waiting a week while he cleared the woolly bunch out of Amarillo so's the next man found a nice, easy town."

"Well, he aims to do it here. And he's too old for it. The cowhands laugh at him, make fun of him. He still goes back, trying to tame them down. Tonight the crews will be in; it's their pay-day. You'll see what I mean."

Red looked at the girl, reading the misery on her face. She'd seen her father and brother die with a law badge on; and her mother shot, carrying ammunition to Stomp Hollorhan when no man would go and help him. Now she was seeing the tragic wreck of a really splendid career. The old man was a mocking-point for the cowhands—who meant nothing by it—except that it was their way to show disrespect for law and order.

"If he just showed them the once that he was as wild and ringy as ever, they wouldn't give him no more trouble at all," Red remarked, half to himself.

"I know that. They're not bad boys for the most part. Brock was the worst. He lived on his brother's guns. And, Red—Jack Brocksen's fast; very fast."

Red accepted this without question; Tildy Mae knew what she was talking about, having seen most of the fast Texas men in action. Red himself was good with a gun; but, under no circumstances, would he call himself fast. To be fast, a man must be able to draw, shoot and hit his mark in under half-a-second. It took Red twice that time to do it.

"Who'all's this Brocksen?" he asked.

"Foreman of the Cooke ranch. Foreman because there isn't another man dare try and stop him. He spoiled his brother and he killed two men who Brock got sassy with and licked by at different times. After that, nobody dare say anything to Brock."

The jail door was thrown open and Tad Cooke came in. His face was flushed and he was breathing hard, as if he'd been running.

"Bill, the hand you knocked down, Red. He's got his horse and is going to tell Brocksen you've killed his brother. I tried to stop him but——"

"Thanks for the warning," Red replied.

"Look, I'm not much of a hand with a gun, but I'll side you. Brocksen won't dare shoot at me."

"Don't be loco, Tad," Tildy Mae snapped. "That killer would down you, or any other man who got in his way."

Tad Cooke looked at the others, then shrugged. "I'm going to try and stop him. In a way I'm responsible for all this."

"Ma'am," Red spoke to Bella. "How about you taking Tad here to your wagon and telling him how much you want for the damage. Then go along to the bank and get the money?"

Bella read the signs and led Tad from the room in a manner which made Tildy Mae smile. Then she turned her attention to Red and asked: "What's on your mind?"

"Doc, you do some mighty good imitations. You reckon you could make me look like ole Stomp?"

Folsom laughed. "It looks easy, but it isn't. Why, I couldn't make myself look enough like anyone to fool people in good light and real close up."

"How about in the dark?" Red answered. "Tildy Mae, has your grandpappy got any more white shirts and vests like that one?"

"Of course, but I don't see how——?"

"I do; the idea has possibilities," Folsom put in. "But it would take someone of my capabilities to put it over."

"We'd have to make sure Stomp couldn't hear us—that'd be the hardest part."

"Not too hard. I carry a certain potion which is guaranteed to make anyone sleep soundly, without doing any harm to them. I assure you, Miss Hollorhan, it is quite harmless." Folsom put this in as Tildy Mae started an angry objection. "I would willingly prove it but haven't the time."

"What do you aim to do, Red?" she asked.

Night came to Pinto City and, with it, the rowdy sounds of Texas cowhands in town for a spree.

In the dining-room of Stomp Hollorhan's small house, Red Blaze pulled the distinctive black-and-white calfskin vest over his white shirt. His wide shoulders strained both to the limit. Tildy came in and smiled. "Nobody will mistake you for gramps."

"It'll be in the dark," Red replied. "Is he sleeping?"

"Like a babe. I don't know what that stuff was that——" she stopped speaking as the door opened and a man came in. "Gramps, what are——? Heavens to Betsy—it's you, Doc!"

Folsom again showed his amazing facility for changing his appearance. The face was lined, seamed and tanned the colour of an old saddle, the eye-brows bushy. In every detail, he was Stomp Hollorhan. All but one, that is. Red was so taken in admiration that he did not notice the gun-belt Folsom wore. If he had, he might have thought even more about this remarkable man.

"Now, who are the main trouble-causers?" Red asked. "We want to know who they are, and where they can be found."

"The Sloanes brothers from the Circle B. They always want to fist-fight with someone. They'll be in the

Alamo. Then there's Dally Dean, three times he's roped gramps and near on every other man in town. His favourite game is to stand just inside the Bull's Head and dab a loop on anyone going by. And there'll be Brocksen. He'll be in town. He uses the Longhorn mostly.''

Red grinned at the girl then looked at Folsom. "You get 'em out into the street and leave the rest to me.''

The Sloanes boys grinned round at their friends from the Circle B. They were watching a bunch of townsmen drinking in the corner.

"Tell you, Benny boy,'' Charlie Sloane said. "That bunch there wouldn't be wuth fighting.''

"Naw,'' Benny agreed delightedly, flexing his muscles. "But there ain't nobody else around for us to fight.''

The saloon door opened and Stomp Hollorhan stood there, just inside. "By cracky, you damned no-good pair. I've telled you afore about starting fights. Now git out here and let's see how good ye are.''

Benny grinned at Charlie. "Old man wants to wressle, Charlie.''

"Shall we oblige?'' Charlie answered. "Long as we watch his brittle ole bones.''

Charlie was the first out; he saw a shadowy figure wearing a black-and-white vest. Charlie stepped forward with a confident grin. A fist like a block of rock smashed under his chin and he reeled back. Benny yelled, and leapt forward.

The door of the saloon opened and Charlie Sloane tottered in. The crowd, including their friends, had heard the sound of the fight. They had been on the verge of coming out to help old Stomp, for they thought the two brothers were going too far this time.

Charlie looked as if he'd tangled with a dozen longhorns; his glassy eyes tried to focus, then his knees gave way. Then the door burst open and Benny sailed in. He landed flat on his back—and stayed there.

In the light of the door, the men saw that angular old shape of Stomp Hollorhan. He set his hat right and growled: "Trouble is, these young 'uns ain't got no go in 'em these days." He paused, then glared round as they had seen him do so many times before. "You Circle B boys behave yourselves."

"Yes sir, Stomp. Yes sir. We surely will!" the foreman replied.

Red Blaze rubbed his knuckles and grinned at Folsom. The Sloane boys were fair fist-fighters, but anyone who'd learned to handle his fists under Mark Counter was more than just fair. Another thing in Red's favour had been that the two young men were over-confident at first; and too groggy to do much about it once they realised that Stomp Hollorhan was still a ringy old cuss.

Dally Dean shook loose the coils of his rope and watched the muttering, grumbling townsman stamp off. He backed into the saloon and grinned at his friend. "Hollorhan's coming," he said. "Watch me fore-foot him."

The others watched, grinning and listening to the sound of approaching feet. Then they saw the familiar vest pass the window. Dean changed his mind and, instead of trying a forefoot throw, sent his loop over the doors to drop round Stomp Hollorhan's shoulders. The young cowhand started to tighten the rope, then he yelled and shot through the door, dragged by a powerful heave. A fist smashed into his stomach, another under his jaw. He howled as the noose was slipped round his arms, the end of his rope thrown up around the outstanding porch support.

By the time the rope-expert's friends recovered their amazed sense and went through the door, Stomp Hollorhan was walking on; and, kicking, yelling, twisting in the air, Dally Dean was hanging with his rope

round his body, and tied so that his feet were well off
the ground.

Red walked on: he was ahead of Folsom, and heard a
voice call: "Stomp!"

Tad Cooke ran up to Red, then stared, his eyes pierc-
ing the blackness enough to know that this was not
Stomp Hollorhan. "Is that you, Red?" he asked.
"Brocksen is in town. He's blaming Stomp for Brock
getting killed."

"Hollorhan!" a voice roared. "Come on out, old
man. I'm going to kill you."

Red saw the big man standing on the porch of the
saloon along the street. He saw, and knew, that Tildy
Mae had been right when she'd said Brocksen was a
good gun. There was that air about him unmistakable to
a man who knew such things. He was in a class that
made Red look slow.

Red was about to move forward when he realised
Folsom was in front of him and headed for the saloon.
The slim man halted in the light of the saloon window
and, in that cracked old voice, asked: "Ye looking for
me, Brocksen?"

"Yeah!" Brocksen stepped from the porch. "I'm
looking for you."

The big man's hand went down. Red was right; he
was very fast. Then Folsom's gun was out, out with that
speed that only a true master ever gained. Flame and
gun-thunder shattered the night. Brocksen stiffened as
lead cut into him. He stood erect for a moment, then
went down in a heap.

Faces at the window of the saloon stared, seeing their
marshal still standing and the fastest gun in town laid on
the ground. Then a man yelled. "Good ole Stomp! He's
the best of them all."

Stomp Hollorhan was in a bad mood when he made his
early morning round. For some reason, he could not

remember a thing after drinking his coffee at dinner. He looked around for the usual signs that the ranch-crews had been in town. Yet there was not a broken window in sight, and there was no line of citizens waiting with complaints. The Sloanes brothers were loading a wagon outside the store, and a man walking along the street bumped into one.

"Why you——!" Benny began.

"Cut it!" Stomp roared, knowing that they would not obey.

Benny turned, saw the marshal and gulped. "Sure thing, Stomp. War only funnin'."

Stomp walked on, wondering if he'd managed to tame the Sloanes boys at last. He was also curious to find out who'd given Benny that swollen nose and the mouse under his eye.

It was further along he saw Dally Dean; but, for the first time, the young cowhand was not carrying his rope.

"See you stopped fooling with that damned riata," Stomp growled.

"Not me, Stomp. No, sir. Not after last night. I'm surely reformed."

Hollorhan eyed the young man suspiciously, but Dally looked quite serious. The old-timer walked on, wondering why everyone was greeting him so respectfully—and how come the cowhands were behaving so politely, instead of hell-raising?

"Stomp!" It was the head of the Town Council and a man who, though a friend, was trying to get rid of the old-timer to put a younger man in office. "You've done it. You've tamed those cowhands down. It was a pity Brocksen had to get killed, but he surely asked for it."

"Should have cleared him out of this section a long time back," Stomp replied. "Town's quiet now though."

"Sure is," the other man showed his admiration. Old Stomp was a modest cuss all right, facing down a man like Brocksen and killing him after whipping the Sloanes boys and teaching Dally Dean a badly-needed lesson. The old-timer certainly had this town fooled. It was a pity that he would be retiring soon.

Hollorhan walked on, shaking his head in wonder, as he was greeted by smiles and cheery nods. It looked as if he'd managed to cool down the hands at last. Maybe he could pull out and settle down on that ranch of his sons.

Tad Cooke, Tildy Mae and that danged whipper-snapper nephew of Ole Devil Hardin were talking to the folks from the Medicine Show in front of his office. He came up and, being a man who made decisions right off, got down to business.

"Tad, you've been shining up to me grand-daughter for months now." He ignored the girl's blushes. "I'm leaving here—going to that spread I bought over San Saba way. Waal, you're a good hand with cattle, but you won't never learn the business working for your paw. If you'd like to come, I'll need me a foreman."

Tildy Mae took Tad's arm, then hooked her other through her grandfather's. She turned and winked at Red and Folsom. "Tell Ole Devil we'll be over to visit him after the fall round-up," she said.

"And tell him to save some of that corn-likker until I come. He never was a judge of it," Stomp growled.

"Wonder if he'll ever find out?" Folsom asked.

"Maybe; maybe not. He'll be leaving here soon, and Tildy Mae can handle him," Red replied. "Talking of handling, where did you learn to handle a gun like that?"

Folsom and his wife looked at each other. Then she smiled, and replied: "We wouldn't want this to get out, but our name isn't Folsom."

"No, we use it as a cover," said her husband. "Find it is less trouble than using my own."

Red watched the man's face. Was there something familiar about it he wondered. "Less trouble?" That was more polite than a direct question.

"Yes, you see my real name is Frank Leslie."

CHAPTER SIX

The Winner of The Bet

"Buckskin Frank Leslie?" Dusty looked at his cousin Red. "I often wondered where he'd got to."

The hour was late and Jean Mollison looked around the table at the men who sat there. She took in Mark's classically handsome features and his giant's size. Then at the Indian-dark, baby-faced innocent expression of the Ysabel Kid. Next, at the freckle-faced, pugnaciously good-looking face of Red Blaze. Then at the intelligent, well-shaped features of the boy she only knew as Waco. Finally her eyes went to the small, insignificant-looking man who was the leader of this reckless bunch of peerless fighting men. The man who led them and steered them through any trouble! Dusty Fog.

"Tell you though," Red went on, having just completed the story of his adventures. "With my kind of luck, I shouldn't be paying in more than six dollars. It was five-to-one that I found trouble."

"You put down the thirty, Red boy," the Ysabel Kid replied unsympathetically.

"The question is, who's won the bet," Jean remarked.

All eyes went to the girl, and the same question flooded into the heads of the men around the table.

"Let me see," Jean went on, ticking the names off on her fingers. "Waco got into trouble in Bennet. The Ysabel Kid found his in the town of Wet Slim. Mark

Counter made it to Casa Grande, then he lost out. Red Blaze, you reached Pinto then you found trouble.''

Dusty reached across the table and took up the money. He tapped it into a neat pile and took the wallet from inside his shirt, opening it.

"Hold hard there, Dusty!" the Kid said softly. "Why for are you putting that money away? You was belly-deep in trouble when we got here.''

"Why sure," Dusty agreed. "What was the bet?''

"That we got to Tensonville without trouble," Mark stated, but there was worry in his voice now.

"What's the name of this town?" Dusty turned to Jean and asked.

"Tensonville," Jean replied, a gurgle of amusement coming into her voice as she saw what Dusty was driving at.

So did the others around the table; and dismay started to show in four faces even before Dusty started to talk again.

"Sure. The bet was that we got to Tensonville, without getting into trouble. That's what I did. Never had any trouble at all until I reached here. Miss Jean, I put it to you, does that cover the agreement we laid down, or not?''

Jean threw back her head, laughing at the mingled dismay and annoyance on the four faces. Then she composed herself and putting on a straight and judicial face nodded her head.

"As an impartial judge, I'd say that Dusty Fog has won the bet.''

WANTED:
Hard Drivin' Westerns From

J.T. Edson's famous "Floating Outfit"
adventure series are on every Western fan's
MOST WANTED list. Don't miss *any* of them!

___THE BAD BUNCH	05228-1/$1.95
___CUCHILO	04836-5/$1.95
___THE FAST GUN	04802-0/$1.95
___.44 CALIBER MAN	04620-6/$1.75
___FROM HIDE AND HORN	04621-4/$1.95
___GO BACK TO HELL	05618-X/$1.95
___GOODNIGHT'S DREAM	04633-8/$1.75
___THE HALF BREED	04736-9/$1.95
___HELL IN THE PALO DURO	05294-X/$1.95
___THE HIDE AND TALLOW MEN	05069-6/$1.95
___THE LAW OF THE GUN	05311-3/$1.95
___THE QUEST FOR BOWIE'S BLADE	05654-6/$2.25
___THE PEACEMAKERS	05529-9/$1.95
___THE TROUBLE BUSTERS	05227-3/$1.95

Berkley Book Mailing Service
P.O. Box 690, Rockville Centre, N.Y. 11570

Please send me the titles checked above. I enclose _____.
Include 75¢ for postage and handling if one book is ordered; 50¢ per book for
two to five. If six or more are ordered, postage is free. California, Illinois, New
York and Tennessee residents please add sales tax.

NAME _____

ADDRESS _____

CITY_____ STATE/ZIP_____

Allow six weeks for delivery.

104 M